Bed Bosh & Beyond

A True Enough Story

H.T. Manogue

Front Cover

Paul Harmon's *The Long Journey*

30 x40" Oil On Canvas

From His 2017: Paintings From The Diary

Doesn't every painter paint his personal journal?

The aspirations and fears.

The soaring dreams and sweet nostalgias.

Well-lighted spaces as well as the darkened corners.

I cannot imagine how terribly sad it would be to look back at one's Body of work

And not see an intimately familiar life.

Other Works By H.T. Manogue

The Lawn Party

The Butterfly Ball

Living Behind the Beauty Shop

Black Orchid Night

Just An Old Fashioned Love Song Meets Stoic Man

Pine Cone Pandemic With Acorn Dressing

Echoes From the Wind

Short Sleeves - Spirit Songs

Short Sleeves - A Book for Friends

Bed Bosh & Beyond

ISBN 10: 0-9778130-6-1

ISBN 13: 978-0-9778130-6-3

www.chortsleeves.net

www.bboshb.com

www.BedBoshBeyound.com

Bob Manogue

Rock On!

1954-2013

Special Thanks To:

Jenny Chandler

Jessica Galbraith

Kathleen Jacoby

Dia Sibert

Janet Riehl

Tom Brown

Cloud nine gets all the publicity, but cloud eight actually is cheaper, less crowded, and has a better view.

George Carlin

It's pain that changes our lives.

Steve Martin

Back Cover

Paul Harmon's The Dance of Life (for Munch)

Oil on Canvas 36 X 48". 2008

From His 2008-2009: Passport Paintings

*In Paul Harmon's longtime attempt to paint
Everything in the world,*

*He discovered early in life that one has to find
Universal icons that
Embrace great bunches of things.*

*And The Passport Paintings are, likewise,
Works in this Quixotesque quest.*

No one knows what's next, but everybody does it.

George Carlin

Those who dance are considered insane by those who cannot hear the music.

George Carlin

Preface

We all move to another dimension of existence at some point in physical life. But we have trepidations about crossing the doorway that leads to this non-physical plane of existence.

We believe the death act is the final bell before the main event. But what is this main event? Religion paints a glorious unified picture of angelic figures and eternal rewards. Religion also paints another portrait that is the complete opposite of our glorious salvation. The Catholics call it hell.

Both paintings hang on the walls of our mind. We adjust the paintings using our beliefs and perceptions, so we achieve our preferred final goal. But maybe, our final goal is not all that final. Perhaps our final goal has several facets to it. And just like in physical life, we can choose what to experience in each of those facets.

In our physical bodies, we function as individuals with our own thoughts, beliefs, and choices. We create a life around the perceptions that suddenly come to life. Perhaps our beliefs and memories don't disappear during and after the death episode. After all, beliefs and memories are not part of our body—they are part of our mind or consciousness.

Our belief about what happens after we pass, is an experience waiting to happen. In other words, if someone believes there is a heaven and hell and a judgment day, they will experience those beliefs for a period that doesn't relate to our physical version of time. If someone believes their actions on earth are more hell worthy than that individual will experience a hell until they make another choice.

No two experiences are the same in life, nor should they be in death. What might be the same is the sudden awareness that we create all of our thoughts, and we logged them in an intricate belief structure. That structure impacts our physical and non-physical life.

There may be a region within the consciousness of death similar to a debriefing area. In that non-physical area, we relive every experience over again in a non-judgmental way. This area is a temporary state where we sense how our beliefs impacted our lives, and the lives of the people we interacted with physically. Once that process ends, we have the opportunity to choose what we want to experience within another region of consciousness.

Everyone has an opinion about death. I believe the first thing we all experience is complete peace. Once we are in that peace, our subjective self examines our objective belief structure. We continue to experience our individual consciousness or mind that connects to the unique consciousness that has always been the whole part of us. That unique consciousness allows every aspect of itself to choose what to experience once our physical life ends. This book is about that choice. It's about beliefs and how they connect the dots in life. And the awareness that appears and continues to expand after what we call death.

H.T.M. – August 2023

Part One

A day without sunshine is like, you know, night.
Steve Martin

Introduction

Pity is for the living; envy is for the dead.

Mark Twain

"It's a blessing and curse to be a light sleeper," he thought.

The aging wood floors and the second floor steps in his Victorian home had secrets to share. And so did every guest who booked a room in his family-owned Bed and Breakfast. He heard more than his fair share of tales, truths, gossip, and secrets over the last twenty-four years. Nothing surprised him anymore—nothing, but the sound death makes when it rings the bell of awakening.

Thomas John Donovan's bell rang a couple of weeks before the official close of winter in 2013. But for some reason his mind functioned as usual, or at least he thought it did. Tom, everyone called him Tom, slowly turned his greying Fu Manchu bearded face toward the night stand and looked at the clock. It was five in the afternoon. Time to get up and finish one of his computer programing projects before he had his signature tomato gravy over pasta dinner with his wife, Dottie. But, something seemed off. He got up, but his two-hundred and fifty- five-pound body stayed in bed. He started floating around the room in another body. He immediately thought about the line his two-year-old nephew, Luke used when he visited Nashville the year before. Luke watched Tom take his usual afternoon snoring siesta on the family living room sofa. The boy smiled and looked up at Dottie as they put Lego's together on the hardwood floor in front of the sofa. LUKE's next words were forever etched in the minds of all family members.

"Uncle Tom forgot to wake-up."

Dottie laughed out loud and woke Tom up. Dottie caught her breath and grabbed Luke and hugged him.

"Uncle Tom's just taking a longer nap than usual, honey. He didn't forget to wake up."

Luke looked at Tom again and smiled.

"You didn't forget to wake up Uncle Tom. You're just tired."

But Tom knew that Luke's words sure fit his current debacle. Tom realized he could still see and could hear. His senses were incredibly heightened.

"This can't be hell." He thought. "But it sure doesn't look like heaven either."

He felt a presence, but wasn't sure what or who it was. Trying to get a handle on his mental state confused him, but the answers seemed to flow through him. He suddenly realized he felt a peace, alert, and joyful state of awareness. Then he heard what seemed to be a voice.

"I guess you know why they call us "Man's best friend, now. Even death doesn't stop us from being close to you."

The voice wasn't a familiar one. He tried to process the sound but couldn't. The voice came again.

"It's us, Tom. It's Wagon, Train, Brando, Dante and Stallone. We want to help you make this part of your life comfortable just like you did for us."

Tom's mind seemed to twirl around space as the voice spoke to him. The dogs spoke, so he could understand them. The woofing and barking of times past turned into cohesive thoughts in this unfamiliar experience.

His eyes caught a glimpse of the dogs standing close to him. They were all wagging their tails.

"God! My life certainly included a series of dogs. If I knew how close you guys are to my maker, I would have fed you better. What are you guys doing here? I know you're not lying around anymore are you? That was your job down there, right?"

"You always said that a dog's life was the best life especially when you moved to California." You said you wanted to see us on the other side and here we are; we're on the other side of the other side. You don't have to worry about diddley squat anymore."

"Where are we guys? Can I be with mom and the rest of the family now?"

"We are in the region of choices, Tom. There's a bunch of places to experience. We call them over-here and over- there."

Tom tried to laugh, and then talk, but the dogs continued.

"Whenever you're ready for them your family will come to you. You can pick to be over-here or over-there. We know you have a lot of questions and you will answer some of them with our help."

"But you know me I would never try to attend the first annual over-here meeting. This is an annual state isn't it?"

"This is an eternal state, Tom."

"I don't know what's in style eternally, and for that matter I wouldn't know what to do about it if I did. Okay, just tell me what I look like now, will ya guys?"

"Well you look like Tom. You don't look like lima beans if that's what you're worried about. We know you don't like Lima beans."

"That's comforting. I guess looking like nothing does have it perks. I guess if this nothing fits I should get another one just like it?"

"You'll have whatever you want here except heaven and hell. That's for religious folks. They will get some of that and some of this too."

"I guess all those California bumper stickers that said: If you can dream it, you can do it. It seems I'm dreaming It now; whatever It is."

Suddenly, the dogs stopped talking, and in the flash of a nanosecond, Tom's birth was front and center. Immediately, Tom realized life and death were two faces of the same ever-changing and eternal coin of existence. Both sides of the coin have distinct features, and both seem valid to the person experiencing them. He felt the loving arms of his mother, as she laid in the stark looking Philadelphia hospital room. The first five years of his life played with him in the same manner. He relieved every experience, and every person in his young life was alive again.

Tom watched himself hold his puppy, King and he felt the warmth of his new friend and thought.

"I wonder if King is in that voice I hear?"

"I'm here too, Tommy." The family called him Tommy was he was a small boy.

A puppy stepped in front of the bigger dogs.

The deep voice sounded familiar but different. Barry White flashed through his mind, but that thought melted when he realized the dog's voice sounded like George Carlin's voice. He watched the next thirty-one years play-out. He experienced his grade school and high school adventures once again. And he began to see how he changed as his beliefs about his experiences changed. Then his short naval experience, his years living in Florida, his early work efforts with his father, and his loved for computers and their programs appeared out of nowhere. Once again his marriage, the birth of his daughters, and buying his first home were front and center in his painless mind His best friends seemed somewhere around him this time. Every person he had contact with was there, and every physical experience played out exactly the way it happened.

He thought again.

"I guess I died by swallowing too much spit over the last fifty-eight years."

He watched himself love, hate, rejoice, fear, and accept what he created in a non-judgmental manner. Each scene danced with brilliance, and the intensity of the self he called Tom.

What he thought of as death gave him the opportunity to examine his life experiences without regret. A sense of calm and contentment wrapped him in a bubble of fullness. He continued to watch the physical side of his coin of existence, and he began to understand the meaning of death.

The death side of his coin was another reality. In that reality, he was like a seed within a flower of knowing. He liked that thought. He started a new chapter in his life, but before he focused completely on that chapter, he realized he would have to relive the rest of his physical years. A sense of calm and contentment wrapped him in this bubble of knowing. And he continued to watch the physical side of his life in a non-universal theater. He was in the region of choice. And he felt the love of those he never thought he would see again.

"Am I a dog now, Wagon?"

The Carlin voice responded.

"You got to wag yourself now, Tom."

Tom liked to say 'sometimes the tail can wag the dog,' when he could speak with his Philly accent.

This story is about that wagging

Chapter 1

"I once spent a year in Philadelphia; I think it was on a Sunday."

W.C. Fields

Tom was now the audience, and the actor in his physical play. Somehow his dogs could show him life scenes. And they sounded like George Carlin. His body screamed young, healthy, and full of vitality. Tom felt like his 1990s self again. He watched himself interact with his mother, Peg. At thirty-six, he started a quest to leave his small hometown just outside Philadelphia, and drive cross-country to start a new job. Unbeknown to him, he would soon be a Bed and Breakfast master.

"I know where California is Tom, but where is this town. What did you call it Hun, Willis?"

"It's Willits mom, and it's in the Northern part of California." Tom grabbed his mother's arm and then hugged her.

"Everything will work out, mom. We'll send you plane tickets."

"You know I hate to fly, Hun, but I guess I'll adjust to it."

"I hope so, Mom. We need someone to fly with the girls to San Francisco. The two of us will drive, but the trip might be a struggle for the girls."

"Tom, you want to drive that old van all the way out there, Hun?"

"It's my duty to find out how much that old Chrysler can take and then push it some more."

"That's a strange way to think, Hun."

"Sometimes a little brain damage helps calm the nerves, mom."

Peg laughed.

"You don't have brain damage, but you do take after your father, you know."

Tom worked for his dad in the braided wool rug business. But her husband's business was on its last leg. Inexpensive imports replaced domestic braided rugs in the major department stores, so new orders were all China bound.

The thought of flying with the girls, and worrying about Tom and Dottie driving that beat-up Van with two huge dogs and a cat started to give Peg a headache.

"The van has what it takes to make it, mom. Don't worry." Tom displayed his signature smile as he continued to tell his mother his plan.

"It's a fresh start for Dottie and me, Mom. The girls are young enough to adjust. Erica is only two, Iris just turned five, and Tiffany celebrates her seventh birthday next month. They say California is a great place to grow up. But I for one will miss my soft pretzels, and my Philly cheese steak and hoagie feasts. Oh, and let's not forget he Philly pizzas and Rolling Rock beer. I need to make some pretty drastic adjustments in my eating habits. I wonder if they serve desert with breakfast out there, mom?"

Tom like to joke with his mother.

"You know what W.C. Fields said about California don't you, Mom?"

"You know I think he's an old wind bag, Hun." Peg's mother use to say that about Fields.

Tom laughed. "You sound like Granny, mom."

"Old W.C. said: California is the only state in the union where you can fall asleep under a rose bush in full bloom and freeze to death. "

I'd say he's got a point, right mom?"

"Oh, Hun you can't hate California because of that old blow-hard, and you can't put down the state because only Philly people know about true Philly cheese steaks. They have orange juice and grapes, plus what about all those beaches. I know you love the shore, Hun."

"It's not the Jersey shore, Mom, and those pale faced hippies get on my nerves. I'll tell you this much; my girls are not going to look like those freaks when they get older. That hippie behavior even pisses the pope off. I think I have just as much authority as that guy. The only difference is not as many people know that."

Peg started laughing. Her son knew how to frame facts into humorous statements even though his facts were not the facts that everyone else accepted.

"I stand by my thoughts, mom. You know you It's pretty hard disagree without being disagreeable, mom."

"Well, let's not bring the pope into this conversation, Hun. You know he's a good soul and our father, dear."

Tom had enough of his mother's religion. He thought it reeked of control and judgment. But he had to play along. He didn't want to upset his mother.

"Yeah, I know you love him, mom, but I don't think he cares if I tell the world that he gets mad just like the rest of us humans. He did have a tough life in Poland, so I know he knows what pissed off is especially when it comes to the Germans and all of their antics. I wonder if things would be much different if Hitler got accepted in art school."

"Don't talk about that sinner. But you know, your grandmother was German, Hun, and she loved the pope."

Tom knew the conversation wouldn't go his way, so he hugged his mother again and looked out the window.

"I know mom. Granny was special wasn't she?"

Dottie suddenly appeared in the next scene along with her parents. She tried to get them excited about the move and where they were going to live. Dottie's parents were staying at their farm in Bucks County.

"Mom and dad said they are going to visit Willits with the Mason's when they go to California tomorrow. They love the Northern part of the state."

Dottie's parents, Jim and Joyce Siebert, had concerns about the move. And they always questioned Tom's abilities. They didn't like the move, but they tried to support it because five-feet two inch Dottie wanted a change.
Dottie personality felt like a package of delightful dynamite. She totally thought the three kids, two dogs, and the cat, welcomed the change as much as she did.

"Do you think your parents should do that, Dot? You know how they are. They might spoil the place before we get there."

"Yes, Tom. We need to find a place to live and they said they would help us. Plus, the Mason's live in San Francisco, so they know all about Mendocino County. The Masons and the Sieberts are like family friends, and I trust them."

Jim and Joyce knew about Mendocino too. Jim, a Notre Dame graduate, grew up in Los Angeles. Joyce, an upper Michigan Peninsula socialite, looked like an older version of Dottie. They bought investment property around LA as well as in other cities. They liked to hunt for ways to increase the return on Joyce's old family money. Jim was a dark haired, blue-eyed Irish FBI agent with lots of connections, so most of their investments became extremely successful.

Jim and Joyce left the small, cluttered living room to see the injured baby bird Dottie rescued from a neighbor's backyard the day before. Dottie loved animals and they loved her.

Tom watched himself whisper in his wife's ear so her parents couldn't hear him.

"Well, I hope they don't stay too long, Dottie. You know they can be annoying."

Tom realized his negativity.

Dottie turned and looked at him. In her best *"what about it, Tom"* voice she whispered:

"Don't start annoying, Tom. What about your dad? He is the king of annoying, right."

"He means well. He is just a little rough around the edges."

Dottie gave him a full-blown knowing look.

"I think it's more than that, but I do like your dad, you know that."

"Everybody likes my dad I think, but he can be a little hard to take at times."

"Remember Tom. The fruit never falls far from the tree."

"You want fruit and we still five steps away from the car. That's all I'll see out there, I guess."

"You're not talking about people are you? That's not the way we talk these days even though your dad might."

"Nah dad's not like that."

His dad, John Tom, had the ability to imagine himself right, and everyone else was wrong. John Tom was John Tom Donovan. Tom realized his father justified his thoughts with distorted emotions.

He heard the dogs' voice again. "Now watch this Tommy. We like this part."

Tom and Dottie hit the road with their two ninety pound dogs, Wagon and Train, and their well-fed cat, Toomy. (Tom named the dogs after his favorite 1960s TV show Wagon Train,) when Jim and Joyce decided to buy the B&B they stayed in the small town of Willits, California. Joyce couldn't resist the six bedrooms, six bath, wood home built at the turn of the twentieth century. In those days, it was the governor of California's summer home.

"You bought what?" The phone in the Motel Six in Arizona cracked as Joyce gave Dottie the news.

"We bought a Bed and Breakfast, Dot, honey. It will give both of you something to do out here. You will love it."

Joyce's words had elements of fatigue, joy, and control in them.

Dottie turned to Tom and whispered.

"Oh my God, Tom. My parents bought a Bed and Breakfast in Willits."

Tom watched himself get annoyed.

"Come on Dot. They didn't really do that. Did they?"

Dottie ignored Tom. Her mind started to percolate, and her words came out like a Japanese bullet train pulling into the next station.

"How are we going to furnish a place like that, mom? You know we're broke."

"Oh don't worry dear. We bought furniture. The place is ready for business. When are you getting here?" Joyce wanted to keep talking, but Dottie cut her off.

"At this rate, late the day after tomorrow sounds about right. Are the kids there yet?"

"Not yet, dear. The Mason's drove down to San Francisco's airport a couple of hours ago. They should be here soon."

"I've got to go, mom. Thanks for your help. At least we have a place to live now. See you soon."

Dottie hung up and looked at Tom.

"Well we got a big house, Tom."

Tom's piercing blue eyes stayed on the road.

"I don't know, Dot. I don't think my first choice would be a Bed and Breakfast. Who will take care of it? I'm not sure our guests will like my scrapple and egg breakfast. Plus, what if I see one of those protected animals on the property eating one of those protected plants?"

Dottie laughed.

"Don't worry, Tom. I don't think downtown Willits has any protected animals or plants. And I doubt scrapple is in grocery stores in Willits. Cooking is my thing. All you have to do is like the place."

"Well as W.C. Fields use to say:

A dead fish can float downstream, but it takes a live one to swim upstream."

"What is that supposed to mean, Tom?"

"I guess swimming upstream is in my future, when I get to Willits."

Dottie smiled.

"If you go swimming, count me in."

Chapter 2

A child of five would understand this. Send someone to fetch a child of five.

Groucho Marx

The urge not to like the Bed and Breakfast jabbed at his brain like a hot poker as Tom drove the old Van on the last leg of the trip to Willits. Tom rattled off several excuses why they shouldn't like their future home, but Dottie had a solution for every one of them.

"If the place only has six bedrooms where will the girls going to sleep, Dot? The guest rooms are for guests. If not, this business is a sinking ship from the start."

Dottie looked at the road sign that read, *Willits 105 miles* and then turned to Tom.

"We are in the dark about this place. Mom said the house has a great back porch and a big attached garage. Maybe the girls could sleep on the porch for a while."

Tom took his eyes off the road, and looked at Dottie.

"You know I love the girls, but I don't want them in bed with us. I need some sleep, not a lot, but some sleep."

"Sure, Tom. We always work things out. We always do."

The new B&B owner kept his foot on the pedal as the road narrowed to two lanes—doing sixty-five in a forty mile an hour zone. Dottie looked at the odometer.

"Hey Tom, I don't want a state trooper to be the first person I meet in California. Slow down."

"What do ya mean, Dot?"

Tom's Philly accent cut the air like fan. It always did when he got nervous. He picked his right foot up, and the car slowed down.

"YO! I heard you say once before that if I'm going slower than you want me too, I'm an idiot, and if I'm going faster you think I'm a moron."

"Sure Tom, I know you know best don't you."

Dottie felt annoyed by Tom's attitude, but she managed to find some humor in it.

"You know what your buddy Groucho would say to you, don't you?" Groucho Marx was one of Tom's childhood heroes.

"What would he say? I'm right, right?"

No, Tom.

"It is better to remain silent and be thought a fool, than to open your mouth and remove all doubt."

Tom laughed and looked at Dottie.

"I thought you were going to say:

"Now there's a man with an open mind — you can feel the breeze from here"

Tom heard the dogs' again. "This place is a dream. Did you ever walk into a room and forget why you walked into it?"

When Tom pulled in front of the B&B, he immediately felt a surge in his energy level.

"Man, look at this place. Look at the garden over there."

She watched as he pointed to the right side of the house.

"Man, there's an attaché d garage over there too."

"I told you that the other night when I talked to mom." Dottie's excitement showed but, so did her slightly annoyed attitude concerning her husband's memory.

"I want to go around this way."

Tom pointed to the left side of the house, but before he could move, the front opened and the three girls came running down the steps. Right behind the girls Dottie's parents, the Mason's, and Peg struggle to keep up.

Tiffany, the oldest, was the first to reach Tom. The other two ran for Dottie.

"What took you so long, Daddy? We thought you be here an hour ago." Tiffany's smile made Tom eyes fill with tears.

"Your mom told me to slowdown"

Dottie heard the comment.

"Tiffany, just be thankful we got here. You know how daddy can be sometimes."

"Grandma Siebert said we might have to sleep on the porch, daddy."

"Don't worry Kiddo; let me see what the rest of the place looks like before we make any of those decisions."

Dottie was excited.

"Come on, Tom. I want to see my new house. Let's see what the inside looks like."

Tom looked up at the flaking paint on the front wood siding, and then looked at the decaying wood porch. The front windows had dry-rot and the beautiful antique door had a missing door handle and lock. Tom knew his life was about to drastically change. His mind raced as the adrenaline flowed through his brain. He found himself knee deep in another world, and that world felt nothing like his Philly cheese steak comfort zone.

He walked into the foyer and stood next to Dottie.

"If the rest of the house needs as much work as the front, we better start saving money, and find some extra help to get this place presentable."

Dottie didn't mind work. When she walked through the door she saw some of the challenges, but she saw a great opportunity as well.

"It's okay Tom. We can do it."

Tom smiled.

"As Groucho said: *Whatever it is, I'm against it.*"

Dottie knew Tom's humor when she heard it.

"Never mind, Tom; let's go upstairs and see the bedrooms."

"Mommy, what about Wagon and Train and Toomy?"

The dogs 'voice came through. "You see how fickle you were. You forgot about us, but we still love you."

Dottie and Tom stopped in their tracks. Middle daughter Iris was the only one that remembered the animals in the car. The dogs just waited for someone to open the back door. The cat, on the other hand, raced back and forth from front window to back window meowing for attention.

Dottie immediately turned around and sprinted out the front door toward the car. She flew down the steps to the street and opened the back hatch. Both dogs got up with tails wagging. The cat immediately ran through the legs of the white German shepherd and ran tail-up to the back of the house.

"It's okay you guys, I got something special for you."

Dottie grabbed a cooler filled with special dog treats. She closed the back van door as the dogs circled her with doggie love.

Inside, Tom brought his mom up to speed on their road trip. Jim and Joyce opened the interior door and walked into the parlor of the turn-of-the-century beauty. The Masons followed them.

"Let's see the bedrooms." Dottie wanted to see how much work she was facing.

Dottie opened the first door at the top of the stairs. The Victorian decorated bedroom was presidential worthy. Without saying a word, she darted across the hall to another larger bedroom furnished in true mid-ninetieth century style. Tom and the rest of the group tried to keep up the pace.

"Yo, Dot. Wait a minute would you? Don't you want to talk about any of this while we see it?"

"I want to see all the bedrooms first, Tom. Then we can talk."

"Well, it would be nice if you slow down. We have plenty of time to see all this. Remember what you told me in the van."

"What's that Tom?"

"You didn't want a trooper to be the first Californian you meet."

"Yeah, right! So what's that got to do with me now?"

"Well, I don't want a doctor to be the first person I meet in California. I'm afraid you're going to have a heart attack with all this running from room to room."

Dottie started to laugh and so did the entourage behind her.

"Oh, come on. You know I'm in perfect condition. I think you just don't want to keep up with me."

"Right, Dot. I have horse sense."

"Horse sense?" Dottie waited for the humor to drop.

"Yeah, you know what Groucho said: Horse sense is the thing a horse has. Horse sense keeps the horse from betting on people."

The grouped laughed as they stood in the narrow hall between the bedrooms.

Dottie looked at Tom.

"Let's go see the rest of the house before your horse sense leaves you."

"Okay, but I'm going first." Tom was the last one in line in the hallway so it was only natural for him to go first when he turned around.

Dottie smiled.

"Good thinking." Peg chuckled as she followed her son down the steps.

"Let's call this place "President's Bed & Breakfast. I love the sound of that don't you? I guess the girls could sleep on the porch for a little while, Tom, but let's go look at the garage. Maybe that would work as bedrooms."

Tom had a puzzled look on his face.

"The name rocks, but I don't know about the garage, Dot? It may get cold, and it's not connected to the house. I really don't want the girls sleeping out there. You know California has all kinds of nuts, and I don't mean the ones that grow on trees."

"Come on Tom let's look anyway. You never know what we can do." Jim and Joyce shook their head in agreement, but Peg added her two cents.

"I agree, Hun. I don't think the girls want to be that far away from you two, Dottie."

Tiffany jumped in the conversation.

"Oh, no worries, Granny. We already looked at the garage and it's filled with junk. We want to sleep on the porch for now. It has lots of windows."

Jim jumped into the conversation.

"I can make three bedrooms in that garage area. Just give me a week, and it will look like a million bucks. I bet mommy and daddy will make that porch a special place while I fix-up the garage."

Tom thought for a minute. "My in-laws have a lot of ideas, but they all suck. All I hear is work and more work for me."

Chapter 3

Liberals can understand everything but people who don't understand them.

Lenny Bruce

Willits, California used to answer to "Willitsville" when Ken Brier founded the settlement on Hiram Willits land in 1857. When the post office opened in 1861, the town got a new name— Little Lake. In 1874, the name changed to Willits.

The city of Willits incorporated in 1888. When Tom and Dottie made their way to what some folks called the "Heart of Mendocino County" or the "Gateway to the Redwoods," it still had that sleepy town mentality and about 5,000 residents. The only noteworthy resident at that time was the deceased Triple Crown winner Seabiscuit. Seabiscuit's grave secretly sits on his training site, Ridgewood Ranch. Labor leader and feminist Judi Bari also had a home in Willits back in the 1990s.

Tom got excited and nervous as his new career as a rug maker for Deluxe Rugs of Northern California started to become a reality. Deluxe owner Max Gutman was a short, plump, red- nose, brown eyed, Jewish business man from Oakland, California. Max was also a divorced, balding, grey-haired conservative that didn't like much of anything

— except his braided wool throw rugs, and his upscale wall-to-wall art deco floor masterpieces.

Tom stood in front of Max and plant manager Frank Rainwater, a member of the Pomo tribe. Frank's face looked like it belonged on a Buffalo nickel. His handsome and very distinct features stood out in any crowd. He still wore a bear tooth necklace around his neck, and his thick black hair was always pulled back in a long pony tail. Frank, the Indian, wore an old Calvary hat. Tom thought the Indian war wasn't over in California yet.

His new boss, Max, delivered his sermon like a garden hose on the jet stream setting.

"You know I don't like any monkey business while you're working, Tom. No web skating or whatever they call it. I expect you to give me your undivided attention. That means all you think about while you're on the clock is how to make money for my factory with that mishegas computing thing. I think your dad told me you learned how to work that thing without any formal training. Is that right?"

"Yes sir, Max. I am self-taught. I know I can help you increase productivity using my computer. What did you call it, Max?"

"Never mind, son. You got my meaning. I don't need you thinking too much. That's big Frank's job. Frank will fill in the blanks. I'm late for another meeting."

Max hurried out of the office like a cop who just got a 211 robbery call. Frank looked down at Tom. Frank's 6 foot-two-inch muscular frame and his compassionate aura made Tom relax a bit.

"Don't worry, Tom. He can be a pain in the butt sometimes, but he is good at business. Just try to stay out of his way. Make sure you talk to me before you do anything that might upset him."

"What might that be, Frank?"

"He's not one for change. I've been here for six years. My first year here you could call a zoo. The workers wanted to quit because Max made them work in the factory without air-conditioning in the summer and without heat in the winter. We didn't have a break room, and the workers had to work every Saturday for regular wage. He wouldn't think about adding a computer program until he saw your dad's operation in Pennsylvania."

"So how did you get him to change?"

"I just told him that this was a 20th century operation not a 19th century hot shop. I forced him to put in air-conditioning and turn on the heat during the cold months. He didn't like it at first because of the expense. But he knew I could get the workers to walk out if he didn't change the hours and give them some modern day perks. Most of the workers are from my tribe."

"Oh, you pulled a Little Big Horn scenario on him. I bet you pissed him off. Oh, sorry Frank I meant no disrespect."

"No worries, Tom. I never looked at it that way, but I guess I did. We circled his greedy wagon train and got him to surrender. We wanted to save him from his own ignorance. The difference between me and the Lakota, Arapaho, and Cheyenne tribes in South Dakota was my choice. They had no choice but to show the white-eyes the result of their ignorance. We tried to save Max from his own ignorant greed."

"Did Max want to fire you?"

"Yeah man. He wouldn't talk to me for weeks. He sent his secretary, Dora, out here to tell me what to do every morning. I finally had to go into his office and have a major pow-wow. I sat down in front of him and told him that he hired me to manage the plant. I told him I was an Indian medicine man with strong powers, not a yes man."

Tom smiled. He liked Frank.

"What did he say when you said that?"

"He started laughing and said I was full of shit. I started to laugh too. He pulled out the shipping figures from the previous two weeks and threw them on top of his desk in front of me. Productivity was up twenty percent. He knew the changes were going to make him more money. Money was the catalyst for him to talk to me again. I got up and started to walk out of his office. As I was leaving he told me he hated what I did, but loved the results. He also told me if I ever did anything like that again he would fire me."

"What did you think about that statement, Frank?"

"Well, I've made several changes since then without his approval, and I'm still here. As long as our production and shipping figures are up, he leaves me alone. He doesn't like it, but he doesn't like much of anything. He's like a hungry wolverine with no friends."

The dogs' voice changed the scene or so it seemed to Tom. "You create a certain amount of madness in your own cleaver way."

Dottie was on the front lawn playing with the three girls as Tom watched his thirty-something self pull the old van into the driveway. His blue dress shirt was soaked with perspiration. As he opened the door and stepped out of the van, he couldn't help yelling at Dottie.

"I gotta get that AC fixed. Man it's hot."

"We got bigger problems, Tom. I took the girls to school today. What a nightmare. Parents brought their kids in barefoot, and their clothes looked like goodwill rejects. The principal needs to tell parents what kind of dress code is in place."

Tom went over to the girls and gave them all a kiss as he listened to the frustration in Dottie's voice. Tiffany pulled away from Tom's sweaty face. Iris told him to wipe his forehead with something. Erica ran over to Dottie after Tom planted a sweaty kiss on her cheek. Tom's frustration suddenly exploded.

"I told you we went back in time. This place is a little unreal. Max told me I am a prisoner in so many words. Thank God for Frank. That's all I can say."

"Prisoner? What are you talking about, Tom?"

"That guy worked as a guard at a German prison camp during the war."

"Tom, Max is Jewish."

Dottie shook her head at Tom's lack of patience. As Tom watched this 23-year-old event unfold again, he understood his wife's frustration.

"Well he acts like one. You should hear some of his Yiddish comments, Dottie. He doesn't know it, but I know a little bit about schmucks too. Did you book any rooms today? We got to get some guests in order to survive out here. I feel like Custer right now."

Dottie looked at Tom. Her annoying button was in the on position.

"Schmuck? Custer? Really Tom? I never thought your first

47

day at work would turn out to be so brutal. But I think you're old enough to deal with this petty stuff. You are old enough aren't you?"

Tom watched his younger self gain some control over his emotions.

"You know the medical profession says that we function using only 10% of our brains The other 90% keeps us from knowing why guys like Max functioning like they do."

Dottie smiled.

"Good! That's the Tom I know. That's the man who defies description. Now, I can start dinner, and after that I can get the house ready for guests. I got two bookings today. One is for Thursday and the other is for Sunday. After dinner you can read the girls a story, and get them ready for bed."

Tom still had the meeting with Max on his mind.

"I don't think Max likes me, Dottie. Frank says he doesn't like anybody."

Dottie rolled her eyes as she picked up Erica and asked the older girls to go inside. She had a smart answer for Tom, but she held her tongue.

"Well, he must not like himself. You didn't bring up Lenny Bruce or Groucho during your meeting did you?"

"Nah, he's just a greedy blow-hard with no principles."

"Tom, you sound like your mother."

"I know. I miss her. A good Philly cheese steak and a bottle of Rolling Rock would help me through this debacle. I don't like the Steelers, but I do like their beer. What's for dinner?"

"Well honey, Rolling Rock hasn't reached Willits yet, so you'll just have to make due with root beer, a salad and a broiled chicken breast I'm fixing."

Tom thought for a minute and then frowned.

"I didn't know the chicken needed fixing They seem to do the job the way they are."

Dottie smiled and rolled her eyes. Tom continued his rant.

"You know I hate salad, Dottie. I'm going down to that sandwich place on Main Street and get us all John Tom burgers and French fries. What's that place called, Dot?"

"It's called Schenks. Tom. But, we gotta start eating like we are in California. I don't want the girls eating greasy food and you shouldn't either."

"It's okay I plan to start working out. Frank says the company has a membership to the gym on South Main Street."

Dottie's next thoughts hit a nerve of remembering.

"I'll believe that when I see it. Tonight let's eat a healthy meal. That way you will be one step closer to being a health nut."

Tom heard the voice of his dogs again. "We liked to bury our meals sometimes."

"But you guys are dogs?"

"Old news, Tommy. Life is life. The idea of difference doesn't exist here. Listen to Koi."

Koi Brightsky was Frank's wife of eighteen years. Her father was the chief and medicine man of the Pomo tribe for over fifty years. Koi also held the title of tribal healer. She didn't look like one, however. Her round tanned face was the perfect canvas for her crystal green eyes and exquisitely shaped nosed. Her full lips complimented her thick dark symmetrical eyebrows. An eagle feather slipped through a large porcupine quill comb in her silky black hair. The comb kept her hair arranged in a side pony tail. Her high forehead and enunciated cheekbones made her look like an Native American goddess. She stood five-feet tall. But she displayed a powerful image wherever she went.

 Koi sat in the lobby. She waited for Frank to come out of a meeting with Max. It was the first time Tom saw a Native American woman in person. He thought she looked like young Natalie Wood in the movie, *The Searchers*. It was his first encounter with someone who lived close to nature.

And he wanted to make the best of it, so he jumped off his stool in the glass enclosed area that Max named his office. He walked up to Koi and put his hand out.

"Hi I'm Tom from Pennsylvania. Frank said you heal people. This is a first for me. Meeting a healer was not in my plans today. Are you a doctor?"

Koi smiled as she put her soft hand in his big right hand.

"My people consider me a doctor."

"How did you train for that job? Did you learn from your parents?"

Koi put her hands together in front of her and looked Tom in the eyes.

"We believe the earth provides everything we need to be healthy. We believe the body can heal itself when the mind is clear. What do you believe?"

Tom saw himself think for a minute. He wasn't sure what he believed.

"I guess I believe what my parents taught me. Sounds like you do too. The only difference is modern doctors took the place of medicine men in my culture. They have powerful medicine I guess."

Koi looked down at her elk moccasin covered feet. She hesitated for a minute.

"We all believe in many things. You believe what your doctor tells you when it comes to taking medicine, right? My people believe I know the right medicine to give them for all their ailments. Your doctors use our remedies and

change them, so they can be produced to make money. We don't mix money and health. Our belief about money does not overlap with our belief about health."

"Oh, I see. You use natural ingredients instead of synthetically re-engineered drugs. Do you get paid for what you do?"

"I do get paid, but not with money. My family and extended family live long healthy lives. They contribute value to our community by offering what they have to give. They all have appreciation and they share it with me. Appreciation is the highest payment in our tribe. There are no attachments within pure appreciation. There is only the powerful energy of thank you within it. Thank you in our language means soul within the gods."

Tom listened and smiled. Koi spoke in clear fluent sentences. Her thoughts made him think about the phrase thank you. Tom wasn't sure what to say so he blurted out:

"A heart-felt thank you does make the soul feel good doesn't it?"

Koi shook her head in agreement, and as she did Frank came out of Max's office. Tom heard her mumbled some-thing.

"ʔa·y ma tana?"

Koi understood the mumble and answered.

"ʔe· ʔa·na?"

Tom looked at both of them.

"I guess I better get back to my office. I only know two languages. English and broken English."

They both laughed as they walked back to Frank's office. Tom went back to his office, so he could get another glimpse of Koi when she left. He liked her. She seemed real.

Tom could see everything in that 5' x 5' office. He called it an office, but it was still a supply room. Tom didn't care. It suited his needs. No one bothered him or came in and sat down. There was only room for one chair, and Tom sat on it. If a worker needed something from Tom, they just stood by the door and asked. He also liked it because he saw everyone that came in and out of the plant unless Max covered the glass window in his office with black cellophane. He did that in the past. Max liked to hide what he called his trade secrets. When out of town guests started staying at Tom's B&B later that year, Max covered Tom's office window with black cellophane, so his guests wouldn't know Tom worked there.

Chapter 4

You're nuts but you're welcome here.
Steve Martin

The first guest was already at the B&B when Tom came home from work around six that Thursday night. He didn't need a watch; his stomach always told him what time it was. Tom walk through the open inside door and saw Dottie and a plump, grey-haired middle-aged woman with horn-rimmed glasses sitting in the parlor. They both had a glass of chardonnay sitting on the table in front of them.

Dottie got up from the soft brown leather sofa and her guest did as well.

"Tom this is Candice Kerns. She plans to stay with us until Monday. I put her in the Roosevelt Room. She came out to see her daughter, May.

Candice smiled and began to speak. When she did, the space between her slightly yellow front teeth became Tom's point of interest.

"Nice to meet you, Tom. I was just telling Dot I love your home. It reminds me of my grandmother's home in Tonawanda, New York."

Tom tried to look her in the eyes, but her big brown eyes seemed to cross when she looked at him, so he turned his attention to the glass in Candice hand as he squeezed out the words.

"Is New York your birth state, Candice?" Before she could answer, he fired another question her way.

"Is this your first time in Northern California?"

Candice sat down as Tom moved toward the red velvet wing back chair across from the sofa. Dottie sat back down. But as she did, she knocked over her glass of wine.

"Oh what a klutz. Excuse me for a minute, Candice." Dottie raced toward the kitchen. Dottie faux pas didn't faze Candice. She looked at Tom with that same interesting smile.

"No, I'm from Staten Island."

Tom stayed confused.

"Staten Island is in New York isn't it?"

Candice and her wicked belly laugh gave Tom the full flavor of it, when she answered him.

"Oh, Tonawanda is actually part of Buffalo. It's New York, but it is a different kind of New York. Ya know what I mean, honey?"

Candice's thick Staten Island accent exacerbated her inferred conclusion. Tom knew he might get into something he might regret.

"I understand Candice. Staten Island is more like New York City, right? They call that Buffalo area upstate don't they?" Upstate is like, laid-back. Right?"

Just as Candice said: "Yep, I guess so." Dottie came back with a damp cloth and another glass of wine.

"Here Tom I'm not drinking anymore. I've got to get dinner ready for the girls. I gave Candice the address of Saldutti's Italian Restaurant I told her how much we loved the pasta primavera."

Tom put the glass down, and looked at Candice— then at Dottie.

"Well, some of us like the primavera. Others like the spaghetti and meatballs with that thick tomato gravy."

Tom felt the air from Candice's belly laugh again. She grabbed her glass of wine and finished off the half glass in one swallow.

"I'll eat anything, honey. Hell, I'm way past hungry. It's nine-thirty my time."

Tom still wanted Candice to answer his original question, and he added a couple of new ones as she got up from the sofa.

"Is this your first trip to California? What's your daughter doing here, Candice? Is she working at one of the vineyards?"

Candice looked at Tom with a sheepish grin, which exposed her separated front teeth.

"No, honey. I was here in '78 with my third husband. He died while we were staying at the Fairmount in San Francisco."

"My condolences, Candice. Was he sick?"

"He choked on a piece of meat in the hotel restaurant."

"Did anyone try to give him the Heimlich maneuver?"

"Well no. I started to choke at the same time. Man, I thought my luck ran out. A guy at the next table jumped up to help my husband, and the waiter tried to help me. And he did, but poor ole Dean had a heart attack while he choked. He left his body in a matter of seconds."

"What a story, Candice. That reminds me of a story that claimed there was an ancient civilization built on nothing but gossip. Was Dean your daughter's father?"

"No honey, Melvin is. I married Mel about a year after Dean passed."

Tom slowly and somewhat sarcastically replied.

"I hope Mel feels okay. What does May do here, Candice?"

Dottie nodded.

"I'm not supposed to tell nobody, but she helps an old high school friend grow pot. You can keep a secret right, honey?"

Candice softly squeezed Tom on the cheek as she finished her sentence, and then she started another one.

"I'll see you at seven in the morning for breakfast, honey. I need a little dinner now. But breakfast is my favorite meal. Dot said she can fix me a special breakfast meal."

Tom nodded his head and smiled. He still had a hard time believing her death story and the pot comment. How could two people choke on steak at the same time? He knew the Mayacmas Mountains were a prime pot growing haven. But he never thought pot growers would get this close to the girls. He followed Candice out the front door, and immediately raced back through the house to find Dottie. Dottie put a salad together in the kitchen.

Tom's nerves hit high gear, and Dottie felt it. "Where are the girls, Dottie?"

Dottie could hear the fear in his voice. "Playing in the garage, Tom."

"Good. Do you know who our first guest plans to bring here tomorrow?"

Dottie had no clue, but she knew she was about to find out.

"I think her daughter is coming to get her after breakfast."

"Right, Dot! Her daughter the pot grower! Is that the kind of guests we expect to get in this city? You don't want to expose our daughters to weed this early in their lives do you, Dottie?"

Dottie knew Tom was in acting mode.

"Calm down, Tom. The girls won't know anything about it. I told Candice that we don't want to be around anything that is illegal. And she assured me that her daughter would not be stoned when she picks her up."

"How is Candice going to control that? Her daughter must be bleeding from the eyes all day long. You know how stoners are, Dottie. We promised each other we stop all that wacked-out stuff before the girls were born."

Dottie looked at Tom and smiled.

"Did she tell you the choking story?"

Tom rolled his eyes.

"She a little off in the head. That choking episode must have cut her oxygen supply off for a while. I don't think she is all there. She likes to marry. I don't know how many times she walked down the aisle."

"Don't worry, babe. The girls will adjust. Why don't you go out to the garage and spend some time with them before dinner? They want to talk to you. I'll make sure Candice and her daughter leave before the girls see them tomorrow. I know what I'm doing, Tom."

Tom felt better as he walked toward the garage. He didn't think about his guest before he met Candice, but now the guests and Max were at the top of his adrenaline list. There was a new guest coming on Sunday. He started to imagine what that guest will do in Willits, but he decided to change his thoughts.

"I wonder why I never see a great looking homeless couple in this town? "

He heard the dogs say. "You could have shaken those pot thoughts off just like we shook after a bath. It's life Tom. You got over that part of it.

Winston Gasper stood at the front door of the old Victorian B&B and rang the bell. It was seven Sunday night. He had travel lag from his trip. Winston left San Diego by bus around four that morning and didn't sleep a wink. He was too busy writing about his quest to see the world on

$50 a day. He was in the third month of his trip, and it turned out much different than he planned.

Tom watched as he opened the door. The young man who stood on the other side of the door was a tall, thin guy with long blonde hair wrapped in corn rolls, and an unruly long dark brown moustache and beard that outlined his tan face. His black backpack had stains all over it, and his madras shorts and white tee shirt looked like they stuck to his body.

"Hi, are you Winston?" Tom looked at him and his mind started forming judgments.

"Yes, sir. I called your wife and told her I needed a room, with no breakfast for thirty dollars, and she said that would be okay."

Winston looked at Tom. He knew he formed his opinion of Winston based on his appearance.

"Come in, Winston." Tom put his hand out. "We have one guest in our front room on the left. You can stay in the Harding Room, which is the second door on the right. Everything you need to make your stay a great one is in that room. Bottled water is in the hall. If you need anything else, let me know. My wife will be back later this evening."

"I appreciate it, Tom. I need a shower and a bottle of water."

Winston almost trip when he reached the second landing, but he regain his balance. Tom heard the Harding Room door open and then close. He went into the parlor and sat in his recliner and grabbed the remote. Wagon and Train came out of his bedroom and found a comfortable place on the floor. The faint smell of dog permeated the room, but he was use to that scent. He began surfing the channels and found the History channel. He wasn't sure what was on, until he saw a group of Calvary soldiers riding full speed on horseback. The soldiers followed a guy with long yellow hair in a buckskin jacket. Immediately, he recognized the guy and the story. It was Errol Flynn in *Custer's Last Stand*.

He heard himself think. "How strange, man? I talked about Custer the other day, and here he is."

About thirty minutes into the program, Winston knocked on the inner door. The dogs immediately got up and began barking. Tom yelled for him to come in.

Winston cautiously opened the door. He liked dogs, but from the sound of the barks these dogs were big.

Tom noticed the hesitation.

"Come in Winston. They won't hurt you."

When Winston opened the door the dogs circled him and began sniffing. He put his hand out palms up and the both dogs began the licking and wagging process. Winston relaxed and looked at Tom.

"Sorry to bother you, Tom, but I have a question."

Tom put the foot rest down on his chair and sat as straight as he could.

"Sure, what do you need? Are you hungry?" Winston smiled.

"No, I'm good, but I would like to watch the CNBC so I get a feel for where the market may start in the morning."

Tom looked out the front window for a second. Custer was getting ready to meet his maker via the Indians, and he didn't want to miss that part. But, Winston was a guest albeit another strange guest.

"Sure Winston. Sit down and I'll turn it on. Are you interested in investing?"

Winston sat in the rocking chair in front of the TV.

"Well, I have a master's in economics from Harvard and have quite an extensive portfolio. I don't pay much attention to it these days. Every now and then I get the urge to see how my money works for me, but I usually turn the TV off or get distracted before I see the information. I guess it's some kind of game I play with myself."

"Do you have a broker?"

"Well, dad handles my money. He gave me stocks when I was a kid. I had a falling out with him, so I pretty much ignore all that bullshit now."

"So why do you want to watch it now? Do you want to reconcile with your dad?"

"Nah, my life style annoys him. He thinks I'm crazy for traveling the world on $50 a day."

"It sounds like that's a very challenging dream, Winston. Where you been so far?"

Winston looked at Tom when he spoke. He never looked at the TV.

"Vancouver. Cops threw me in jail for loitering. I sat in a cell for almost three months before they released me. I met some interesting guys in prison. But I finally decided to make the call home, so I could continue my trip. When I got out last week, I went home to San Diego. Dad bailed me out after a talk with my mother on the phone. That call tested my determination."

"You mean going back home was hard?"

Tom's one nerve surfaced. He wanted to watch Custer get an Indian burr-cut. But instead he listened to what sounded like a young lunatic trying to find some sort of sanity from his insane choices.

"Going home was a bummer, man. My dad tried to get me to stay and go to work for him. Heck, Jail wasn't all that bad. I saved $50 a day while I was in there, so I'm ahead of the game right now. If I went to work for dad, freedom disappears, and hard work becomes a fact. Work means conformity with limited freedom. Who wants that?"

"Hard work? Ahead of the game? That's one way of looking at it, I guess. I think you have to work at some point in your life. It sounds like you can do whatever you want. It's just a matter of finding something you want to do, Winston. Maybe this adventure will help you find yourself."

"Man, I've got a good handle on myself. I know I can be whatever I want to be. At this point, I want to be the me that's free. Free to choose the fun instead of the fear. Free to appreciate the earth and everything connected to it. I am part of this expanding universe. And I want to feel that growth without any man-made restrictions."

Tom suddenly realized he had one of those California hippies sitting in his house. It was one thing to have the mother of a pot addict in house. But bonding with a hippie was way out of his comfort zone. If the first two guests were any indication of what was to come, he was in for some radical adjustments in his thinking. Tom looked at the TV and then at Winston. Winston looked at the books above the TV.

"What next on your travel agenda, Winston?"

"Please call me Win, Tom. Off to Seattle and then flying to Bangkok. I want to make my way through Asia, Europe, and South America."

Tom wanted to end the conversation, but he still had questions.

"How long is this adventure going to take, Win?"

"As long as it takes, man. Time is on my side."

Tom was out of questions and patience. All he could say was a phrase he heard someone say in a movie.

"I wish you luck, and Godspeed."

Winston smiled at Tom.

"Tom there ain't no luck, and there ain't just one God. But thanks anyway. I'll see you in the morning."

"Okay, Win thanks."

Tom didn't want to see Win again. He was everything he hated rolled up in one person. He hated Winston's freedom. He hated his ability to express himself without conforming, and he hated his attitude toward life.

Chapter 5

You're only given a little spark of madness. You mustn't lose it.

Tomin Williams

By the time Dottie got home Tom had enough. Their first two guests were more than he could handle. They represented some of the issues that made Tom suspicious of California. When Dottie opened the interior door to the parlor she heard Tom on the back porch. He was on the computer. The dogs immediately got up from their favorite place on the porch and hurried toward the sound of the girls. When Dottie reached the porch Tom looked up and began his preconceive speech.

"This guest is just as kooky as the first one, Dot."

Dottie held up one finger to her mouth and whispered.

"We'll talk later. Let me get the girls in bed. They have school tomorrow. Girls, give daddy a kiss it's bedtime."

The girls ran up to Tom. They gave him a joint family goodnight hug and kiss.

"Sleep tight girls. I love you. I'll see you in the morning."

In perfect harmony the girls replied. "Night daddy we love you too."

Dottie started a Shel Silverstein book, but the girls were asleep before she could turn to page four. Dottie was back on the porch within thirty minutes. She stood by her husband's desk and started to yawn.

"So what about the new guest? Is he a mass murderer or something?"

"He's a hippie with a Master's degree in economics! That's almost as bad. Where did you get these guests? It seems like they suddenly appeared to annoy the hell out of me."

"Everything annoys you; your job, the girls, the guests, the dogs, the cat and my family. By the way, Hazel wants to come next weekend with Todd, Eddie, and Lois."

He heard the dogs again. "You see how hard you made life?"

"Oh geese! That means a full house. Forget making money, if your sister starts hanging around every weekend with her kids? And besides that she's as crazy as our two guests."

"I don't want to talk about all this now, Tom. Let's get through the week. We got a judge coming in on Tuesday and a nurse on Wednesday. I think they will suit your judgmental nerves a little better."

Dottie started to walk toward the kitchen door. Tom was still in conversation mode.

"Oh by the way, how did your meeting go with the Doyle's?"

"It was nice to be around a normal family for a change. The girls and I really hit it off with them. They want us to come over for dinner Friday night."

"Okay Dot I'll go. But just so you know, the girls and the dog don't annoy me."

The Doyle's were a well-respect family in Willits. Barbie Clark Doyle taught second grade at Willits Elementary School. And Jack Doyle owned the Co-op in town. Their daughter Riley was Tiffany's age, and son Jackie was Erica's age. Tiffany and Riley bonded quickly after the first week of school. Barbie wanted to meet the other members of the Donovan family, so she invited them to her beginning of school family ice cream social. The families clicked immediately. Barbie and Jack Doyle became loyal family friends.

The dogs spoke again.

"Humans are animals too. They're the bargaining kind of animal. We never shared bones with other dogs."

Tom felt the humor and continued to watch his life. His interaction with the feisty old Judge Darren Canfield. And energetic nurse, Katarina Eddy was always a piece of work. Both would visit the B&B numerous times over the next ten years. They became family friends and loyal guests.

Hazel Gilbert, Dottie's oldest sister, was the constant return guest. Hazel had a jealous bone, and she showed it when she visited Dottie's home and family. She did her best to bring aggravation and bullshit to the B&B every time she visited. And her son and daughter did nothing but complain about where they slept and what they ate.

Eddie was a carrot haired, green eyed, chubby kid who lied about everything. He was a year older than Tiffany. And Lois was a year younger than Iris. Her blue eyes, light brown hair, and perfectly shaped oval face got her whatever she wanted. She seemed smart, and uncontrollable. Both kids knew nothing about manners, Temper tantrums got the job done for them. Tom had a hard time interacting with Hazel. and when Todd Gilbert, Hazel's husband, came around Tom had hold back some of his comments that create tension. Todd, a Silicon Valley geek, loved high tech drama but hated normal human interaction.

Tom and the dogs watched one weekend when the Gilbert family and nurse Katarina visited.

Katarina, a thirty-something traveling nurse with dramatic features, was a dead ringer for a young Lauren Bacall. Katarina lived in Hot Springs, Arkansas with her two Shih Tzu's. Willits General Hospital needed more staff, and Katarina loved that part of California. She also loved the B&B and the family. She especially liked Tom's sense of humor. Katrina sat on the leather sofa late one Saturday afternoon, and Hazel and Todd sat in the red winged back chairs. Dottie was in the kitchen and Tom was up to his neck in work on his computer.

Hazel sipped on a Bloody Mary and Todd nursed a double shot of Black Label scotch. Katarina had a glass of sparkling water on the table in front of her.

Hazel looked at Todd. She never acknowledged Katarina.

"I hope those monster dogs are in the garage. The smell kills me, Todd. I'm going to tell Dottie to keep them out of here while we are here. They are just too big to be inside dogs, plus they need a bath. Katherine, you must feel the same way don't you?"

Katarina looked at Hazel. She saw a thirty-five-year-old, overweight, Palo Alto woman that vaguely resembled Dottie physically. She immediately surmised that Hazel would rather complain than agree with anybody.

"It's Katarina not Katherine. No. I think the dogs play an important role in the family."

Todd took a healthy sip of scotch and looked at Hazel. He didn't acknowledge Katarina.

"I think you're right, dear. Next time let's bring Toby with us, so they can see what a house dog looks like."

Toby was the Gilbert's white miniature poodle.

Tom made his way through the dining room when he heard Todd's comment. He couldn't resist jumping into the conversation before he reached the walnut gentlemen's chair by the door.

"I wonder if other dogs think poodles are members of a strange religious doggie cult."

Hazel's white complexion turned red as she put her drink down.

"What on earth do you mean, Tom?"

"You know I love dogs, but if you bring that little knotted-haired cult dog up here, I won't be responsible for what happens to him."

"Nothing will happen to our baby."

Tom smiled, and so did Katarina. Katarina knew Tom always tried to get under her skin.

"Well, you know old Wagon here eats dogs that size for breakfast."

Todd took another sip. He stared at his brother-in-law, but addressed his wife.

"I'll protect Toby, honey. I guarantee that."

Tom's laugh almost shook the room. He looked at Katarina and winked.

"How are you going to do that, Todd? You have a hard

enough time protecting yourself from your wife and kids. They crap all over you, and you sit there like a cow-patty and take it."

Todd didn't know what to say. In a way, he knew Tom had a point. Hazel married him for money. That was no secret.

Hazel made no bones about marrying Todd to get a share of that wealth. Todd's bloodshot eyes focused on Tom.

"You don't have to be so damn cynical, but I guess all wonks are."

Tom pulled on his newly grown brown mustache.

"What's a wonk, Todd?"

Before Todd could answer Hazel chimed in.

"No need to figure it out, Tom. Your manners and your attitude need a serious adjustment. Thank God you married Dottie. At least she has some semblance of manners."

Tom's emotions started to boil. Tom thought a wonk was one of those aliens in Star Wars. Before Tom could take another verbal swing at them, Dottie walked into the room.

"It sounds like you all need to relax a bit. We all be family, so be civil shall we? Katarina please excuse my family's lack of control. I'm sure you know what I mean."

Katarina enjoyed the exchange. She didn't like the Gilberts. They were not her kind of people. She smiled at Dottie.

"I understand, Dottie. I rather enjoy conflicts. They remind me of my childhood years."

Later that night Tom, Hazel, Todd, and Dottie sat down to a roasted chicken, green bean, and potato supper with the fresh green salad Dottie prepared after she fed the kids. The meal was not one of Tom's favorite meals, and the company was not that special either. Hazel put her glass of burgundy to her swollen lips and took a huge gulp. As she put her glass down, she turned to Dottie.

"Do you know what my husband asked Lois and Eddie the other day, Dot?"

Dottie did not want to hear anything Todd had to say, but she acted alert and responded.

"Did he ask them when they were going to start to behave?"

Hazel displayed her disgusted look, which was a basic expression personified a bit.

"No, smart ass. He asked them what color my eyes were. We have been married for over ten years, and that man doesn't know the color of my eyes."

Tom started to laugh. It was one of those inappropriate laughs that make people uncomfortable. After what seemed like one minute of table thumping joy Tom, gained his composure and joined the conversation.

"What did the kids tell him?"

"Hazel looked at Todd. Todd finished his glass of chardonnay and tried to laugh at the same time.

"The kids said they didn't know. Dot, my family doesn't know what color my eyes are, and I'm really pissed about that."

Tom couldn't help himself. He started laughing again and turned to Todd.

"Todd, why the sudden interest in Hazel's eyes? Are you writing a book?"

Todd felt uncomfortable. He grabbed the bottle of chardonnay from the silver ice bucket and filled his glass before he answered.

"I had to fill out insurance papers, and the form wanted to know her eye color. I had a mental block, I guess. I know she has green eyes."

He looked at Hazel and smiled. Hazel shook her head in disbelief.

"Todd you can be such a dumb ass. Why do you think my parents named me Hazel? We don't have any Hazel's in the family. They don't have any friends named Hazel. And there are no Hazel's in the bible except the mention of a hazelnut tree in Genesis 30:37."

Tom couldn't resist.

"You know your bible, Hazel. I'm impressed."

"More people should pay attention to the word of the Lord, Tom. That's what's wrong with this country. We let all these heathens tell us how to live. I for one, place myself in the hands of the Lord. I read the bible every night."

Dottie started to feel nervous. The dinner conversation seemed headed in the wrong direction. She had to change the subject.

"Hazel, are you going to go back to the farm for Ruth's birthday. Mom said the party is June 26th." Hazel looked at Todd.

"I doubt it. Todd has to work, and the kids have swimming lessons. Plus, I have bible study on the 27th"

Todd chimed in.

"We can go Hazel. I'll take a few days off, and the kids don't have to start bible study on that day. We can be flexible if you want to celebrate with Ruth."

Hazel wiped her lips after finishing her third glass of wine. She threw the printed paper napkin on her China plate.

"No Todd. My plans stay the same. Ruth manages fine without us. She probably will have another one of her long string of lovers with her, and I am not interested in meeting any more riff-raft."

Tom found his opening.

"As Groucho use to say: I guess those are your principles and if we don't like them. . . Well, we know you have others."

Hazel didn't laugh. As she walked away from the table, she poured another glass of wine and then sneered at Tom.

"Very funny, Tom. I know you don't get it. Change feels like hard work for me."

As Tom walked into the kitchen he got the last word.

"Everything is hard work for you."

Todd quietly agreed with Tom. Everything seemed like hard work for Hazel. She wanted an easy life, but she made everything difficult.

Chapter 6

I saw the movie, 'Crouching Tiger, Hidden Dragon' and was surprised because I didn't see any tigers or dragons. And then I realized why: they're crouching and hidden.
Steve Martin

The dogs spoke again. "Look at you—clipped and trimmed. You look like a show dog!"

The American dream came true for the Donovan's. After two years with the company, Tom received more responsibilities and more money. But Max was still the same Max. The B&B became the place to stay in that beautiful area of California. Judge Canfield was a regular guest. He often stayed for weeks at a time in order to hear cases in Ukiah.

Judge Canfield was in his early sixties. His judgeship took a toll on his physical appearance. His deeply wrinkled face, and his drooping eyelids drooped over his blue eyes made him look ten years older than dirt. The gray hair that went around his head stop at the top of his ears, so he always wore a white Panama hat.

His five feet nine frame carried 225 lbs. of deteriorating muscle and home grown fat. The judge was a formidable character, even though his appearance was not that menacing. It was his deep, to-the-point voice that made people pay attention to what he had to say. His scholarly voice made everyone stop and take notice. The judge sat at the dining room table dressed in his wrinkled, black and white sear-sucker suit, and black bowtie one Thursday morning with another guest. Dottie and Tom worked in the kitchen.

Dottie put a batch of honey oat muffins on the table as well as a two large crystal glasses filled with a fresh strawberry smoothie. Dottie was in the process of finishing her classic breakfast burrito filled with egg whites, turkey sausage, feta, and spinach. She also brewed a pot of hazelnut coffee. She turned and looked at Tom.

"I think of Hazel every time I brew this kind of coffee. I hate to say it, but it almost makes me sick."

Tom made an annoying face.

"Let's not bring up your sister so early in the morning. I want to help you. I do believe in equality for everyone no matter how stupid they are. But in your sister's case I'll make an exception."

Dottie laughed.

"I guess I shouldn't tell you this, but my sister Ruth wants to come next week."

Tom put his hands over his eyes.

"Well, I have to say she's not as stupid as Hazel, but she's in the race. Thank God your two brothers don't visit. We would sink in the quicksand of Siebert insanity with no life line— and so would the B&B!"

"Okay that's enough Tom. I'm trying to get this breakfast on the table. Go see if the new guest wants another smoothie."

The new guest was Marvin Robbins. Robbins was a Southern California native. He visited Willits for business. No one knew what his business was, but the judge had a hunch. The judge was the first to speak.

"Dottie told me you live in Brawley, California. It's nice to finally meet someone from Brawley. The only thing I know about the place is it gets hot, and it sits below sea level."

The judge knew a lot more than he said about Brawley and his breakfast companion.

Robbins took a sip of his smoothie and grabbed a muffin from the table. He broke it in half with his hands. He stuffed almost a whole half in his mouth, and then washed it down with the smoothie. Robbins wiped the side of his mouth with two fingers and then looked at the judge.

"Yeah, that's right, but we also got two rivers that pass through town, The Alamo and the New."

Robbins took another sip. He didn't want to continue describing his small city. He lived there because it was small, and everybody kept to themselves. He wasn't sure why he even sat down with another guest. He wanted privacy, especially that morning.

The judge felt Robbins aloofness. Robbins demeanor confirmed Canfield's suspicions. His breakfast partner was the man in the papers. The judge put two and two together and spoke again.

"Are you in the horse business, Marvin? You look like you might be a jockey or a trainer."

Canfield picked up a piece of muffin slapped it with a generous amount of butter, and put it in his mouth. Robbins didn't want to answer, but he did.

"What do you do, sir? I know Tom called you judge. Are you a judge?"

The judge smiled.

"Yes, I am. I'm here to hear a very important case. It starts tomorrow. Are you connected to the Ridgewood Ranch?"

Robbins couldn't believe it. Somehow the judge had figured it out. But Robbins wasn't going to give up any pertinent information about his personal life. He experienced that kind of treatment daily in Southern

California.

"I'm here to watch a thief get what he deserves, judge. The guy on trial is my third cousin, Martin Clark. I never liked him. He worked for a short time at Ridgewood as a stable hand. But his personality and addictions were too much for the owners to take. I got him the job, but they let him go after two weeks. My cousin was an angry man. He always wanted to be a jockey, but at 5'5" and 130 lbs. he had a hard time riding to win. He never got over the fact that I was a jockey, and he shoveled horse crap for a living. He drank for twenty-nine of his forty-five years and use drugs to offset his perpetual hangover. He felt jealous of me, and every other jockey. He hated himself and everyone in his life. I want to see him get what he dished out all these years."

Robbins took a deep breath, looked at the judge and started again.

"Yeah, I'm a retired jockey. I still do some training, but I'm not up here to train. I'm here to see justice in action. I guess you're the justice, right judge? Anybody that would steal horses from Ridgewood should be put away, kin or no kin, right?"

Before the judge had a chance to answer, Tom came in with two full plates. The breakfast burritos smelled delicious. When Dottie put the hazelnut coffee down in front of her guests, the aroma made both of them want to dig

82

right in. The judge picked up his fork and looked at Robbins.

"I read the legal documents about your cousin, Marvin. He seemed to made his life difficult from the choices he made."

Robbins thought about the word choices.

"You're right, judge. We all do that guilty thing, don't we?"

The judge swallowed a mouthful of burrito and took a sip of coffee.

"You know it, son. We create a heaven or a hell in the choices we make. I know you know about that."

The judge looked down at his plate and took another sip of coffee. Tom overheard the conversation and came into the room. He wanted to know more about Robbins, but he knew now was not the time to question him, so he changed the subject.

"Dottie said you're going to be staying here all this week, Marvin. Do you need any info about the town?"

Robbins finally wiped the smoothie mustache from his face with his napkin.

"Nah, I've been coming up her for years, so I probably know more about this place than you do."

Robbins didn't smile or say thank you. He just got up, and walked through the parlor and out the front door. The judge got up and looked at Tom.

"That guy has some story, Tom. I read about him last year. He killed his wife's lover and got away with it. I think you better keep an eye on him."

Tom smiled at the judge.

"How did he beat a murder rap in this day and age, judge?"

"Well, it's beyond me, but he did. The incident happened about two years ago. Robbins was in bed one night. He broke his back when thrown from a horse at the Santa Anita Race Track two years before. He was on medication for pain and insomnia. He was also on his fourth wife. He married this last one a year after his injury. They never consummated the marriage due to Robbins inability to have sex and her perpetual excuse making.

She was twenty years younger.

Well, this particular night Mr. Robbins forgot to take his meds and woke up around midnight. He heard his wife moaning and then half screaming in the living room. Robbins didn't know what to think, so he grabbed his .32 colt and walked down the hall. His wife and a man were having some hot sex on the living room sofa. The man was on top, so Robbins fires a shot and hits the culprit in the shoulder. He fell off of the wife and hit the floor. Robbins fired another round, and it hit the man in the stomach. Just to be sure Robbins fired another round, and it caught the guy right between the eyes."

Tom thought for a minute.

"What did his defense claim?"

"Robbins claimed he thought the guy broke into the house and was in the process of raping his wife. He said he tried to protect her, and it was his right to do so. The defense claimed he pulled the trigger in self-defense."

"Wow! I learn something new every day, but I guess this stuff is not new to you. It's old stuff for you, and it's new to me, so I didn't learn something new I learned something old. He shot him three times. What did the wife say about the attack?"

The judge smiled.

"This is where it gets really interesting. The wife said the guy was an old boyfriend. They were having regular sex sessions in Robbins home. Sometimes Robbins was home during these meetings. She told the court that she tried to break it off, but she couldn't."

Tom's eyes showed his confusion

"Robbins killed her boyfriend. Why no conviction?"

"The jury believed Robbins when he told them he never consummated the marriage because his wife was not interested in sex. When Robbins saw his wife screwing another guy, he immediately thought it was an intruder.

The jury acquitted him on all counts in less than twenty-four hours."

"Is Robbins still married to this woman, judge?"

"Yes, that's another fascinating part. Robbins told the press he didn't trust her, but wanted to stay with her. He loved her even though she lied to him."

"You know judge I think you're the only sane guest who stays here. Now we have a murderer staying here. I guess I'll put my .32 under my pillow tonight."

"No need for that, son." The judge put his arm around Tom.

"I know, Judge. He's won't pull anything around here. If he does I'll let Dottie's 70 lb. turtle take a bit out of him."

The judge and Tom laughed.

"Where is this turtle? I want to make sure he can't walk up the front steps and take a bit out of me."

Tom laughed again.

"Oh, don't worry. He only goes upstairs at night. He sits on the second floor back porch and catches bugs."

The judge seemed skeptical. But he was always seemed skeptical. Thirty years on the bench made him that way.

"You have a big turtle that sits on the back porch and catches bugs? I guess the next thing you're going to tell me is you have a bunch of chickens that lay blue and green eggs every morning."

"We do judge, plus we have an herb garden, and I am especially proud of my tomato plants. Come out back, and I'll show you the rest of the family."

The judge stood in the garden and couldn't believe his eyes. Tee-Rex, the massive tortoise, stood in front of him eating a mixture of lettuce, grass, and flowers. Canfield looked over at the chicken coop.

"You guys have a regular farm right here in town. I guess I shouldn't be surprised. You have quite a creative family."

"Thanks, judge. We try to be as self-sufficient as possible. The B&B produces a little money, but I think I'm going to start my own computer business. I want to write programs for people in town."

A year later, Tom started writing new programs for the city of Willits.

"I am quite sure now that often, very often, in matters concerning religion and politics a man's reasoning powers are not above the monkey's."
~ Mark Twain

Chapter 7

Fighting for peace is like screwing for virginity.
 George Carlin

In Dottie's younger days, she always considered Hazel and Ruth, wiser and smarter because of the age difference. Ruth had the real smarts in Dottie's mind because her jet black hair, blue eyes, and creamy white skin made her look the part. Plus, those features confirmed her close connection to her smart Irish dad. But as the years past, Dottie's opinion of Ruth and Hazel changed dramatically.

 In 1995, Ruth had three inches, and twenty pounds on Dottie when she came to stay at the B&B. It was a Saturday in the middle of June. She loved California, but her East Coast roots kept her from moving.

Ruth gave everyone a hug in the foyer when she finally got her three suitcases, purse, and shoulder bag out of the car. Even Tom got a quick squeeze from his sister-in-law. Dottie felt the excitement when she saw Ruth, but her excitement quickly turned to annoyance when her sister opened her mouth.

"I hope you got rid of the dogs Hazel told me about. She said they are too big to be house dogs. She also said you should give me that big room at the top of the stairs."

Dottie fired back before Tom had a chance to open his mouth.

"The dogs are part of this family. If Hazel doesn't like them she can stay home. I don't ask her to come up here and lay around for eight days a month. I've got a business to run. And it's about time she realizes she creates a lot of stress around here."

"Whoa! I didn't mean to expose one of your nerves, Dot. You know I like your dogs. I guess they are up in years by now?"

Dottie settled down.

"Wagon's eleven, and Train is ten. Both of them have hip dysplasia, so they don't get around much anymore. I worry about them. The vet says they may only have a year to live. That thought kills me."

"I know your dogs are the only things that love you more than you do, Dot. Just kidding sis! I'm surprised Hazel even has a dog."

Dottie laughed. She liked Ruth's weird sense of humor.

"The only reason she has a dog is because we have dogs. She wants to show me that she can train animals like I do. But the truth is her dog still pees in the house, Ruth. You know how Hazel Lies."

"You bet I do. She lies to herself and thinks she's fooling everyone around her. We know she's a money hungry bitch who doesn't take responsibility for her words or actions."

Tom had to make a comment.

"That's what I like about you. At least you know your sister. She lives the American dream, but she only realizes it when she's asleep."

Ruth laughed.

Dottie knew the conversation would only go downhill from there.

"Well enough about Hazel. You are in the Taft Room at the top of the steps. The girls put your bags in that BIG room Hazel told you about. We have two other guests. You might meet them later. One is from Michigan, and the other one is from Ohio. They both stayed her before."

"Wow. It sounds like the B&B is a success."

"We are as busy as we want to be. It's a full time job for both of us. That's why Tom gave his notice at the carpet factory. He plans to work from home."

Ruth smiled at Tom, and then she gave him a dose of her dry humor.

"What do you like to do, Tom? Make beds and do laundry."

Tom kept his mouth shut. He knew Dottie would come to his defense.

"Come on, Ruth. Tom hasn't changed that much. He plans to give computer lessons and write computer programs."

"I didn't realize you knew so much about computers, Tom. I knew you knew more than me, but not enough to teach. Maybe you can give me a couple of lessons while I'm here."

"I don't think there's much I can teach you"

Ruth looked up at the foyer chandelier.

"You could start by explaining why prostitution is illegal. Hell, selling is sure legal and screwing is certainly legal. Why is it illegal to sell something we always give away?"

Tom saw an opening.

"Don't tell me you've changed professions, Ruth?"

The dogs' voice became very clear. "A day without a laugh is a dreary day."

Dottie changed the subject.

"Let's go to the store and get what we need for the coming week. You might want to rest a little before we have dinner."

"I do need my rest. I was thinking about all the wine, and all the guys making that wine on the drive up here."

"Ruth, women make wine too. I hope you skip making an ass out of yourself during your stay. It's a small town, and we know a lot of people. People here like friendly, laid back, and liberal visitors. Plus, they like religious folks. They can be pretty nasty if they think you like to sin."

"Hell, sis I'm no sinner. I'm a lover."

"That's what I mean, Ruth."

That evening Ruth never came to dinner. Dottie heard movement on the second floor, but she thought it was the other two guests. The guest from Ohio, Gary Pinner, was a forty-year-old marketing executive. He was in the process of divorcing his second wife. Sunshine Dotson, the guest from Michigan, was on vacation. She was a beautiful, gay, thirty-five-year-old that just broke off a five-year relationship. Somehow Ruth introduced herself to the pair before they went to dinner, and one thing lead to another. The group never made it downstairs. They had a special dinner in Ruth's room.

Tom heard talking and loud laughter coming from the second floor, but the noise stopped right before he went to bed, which was around 2:30. He knew Ruth was up to her old tricks. He mumbled to himself.

"It's a strange world. We tell pregnant women not to drink, but we don't tell sex maniacs not to fuck."

Gary and Sunshine came down and had breakfast together. Ruth stayed in bed. While the pair enjoyed the semolina pancakes and blueberry smoothie, they filled Dottie in on some of the previous night's shenanigans.
Dottie's temper hit the boiling zone, but she kept her composure. She didn't know all the details, but she heard enough. Dottie and Tom decided to confront Ruth when she came down for breakfast. The two guests would never stay there again, but Ruth was family.

When Ruth came down for breakfast it was almost 11:00. Dottie and Tom where still at the table when she sat down.

"Ruth our guests told me about your party. We feel sick about it. Do you know what Gary said? He said *your sister was the one that instigated the party. We thought you guys wouldn't object to us having a little fun.* I told him our house was not a sex den. Do you have any idea what you did, Ruth? Our reputation is at stake."

Ruth picked up the cup in front of her. The cup started to shake as she took a sip.

"Come on, Dot. Just a quick party sis. Everybody enjoyed it." Tom couldn't keep his mouth shut any longer.

"You got to be kidding me, Ruth? I don't care what you think. This is our business, and when you are here you must abide by our rules. That means you can't fuck the guests!"

Dottie looked at Ruth.

"He's right, Ruth. You have to promise me you will not intermingle with the guest unless we are around."

Ruth got up from the table.

"I'm going back to bed. You too are no fun."

Dottie felt relieved. She turned to Tom as she cleaned up Ruth's mess.

"Well thank God the guests arriving tonight are on their honeymoon."

Tom looked up at her and smiled.

"Yeah, let's hope they are not lesbian honeymooners."

"Oh, shit, Tom. I didn't think about that."

Frank and Koi hosted a farewell dinner party for Tom at their home near Sherwood Valley Rancheria the following Thursday night. Dottie and Tom wanted to see how the couple lived. Tom heard rumors about their native life-style. Sherwood Valley Rancheria was the Pomo Indian Reservation, but Frank and Koi's home was not on the

Reservation. It was about 3 miles off highway 101. When they pulled up to the 1960s California ranch style home, the Donovan's could tell they were in for a treat. As they walked up the Mexican tile walkway, they commented on the plants and flowers in bloom. When they reached the 9-foot walnut front door, Tom grabbed the cast iron knocker and hit the doorplate two times. Within thirty seconds the door opened, and a spacious marbled foyer with a hand carved walnut and bone chandelier appeared. Two copper scones sat on each side of a massive redwood wall mirror and entrance table. The carved mirror's frame had Pomo Indian symbols around the edge. Frank and Koi stood in front of the table.

Frank extended his hand to Tom, and Koi reached over and hugged Dottie. Frank spoke first.

"Welcome to our home. You are our honored guests, and the first guest to arrive. Please, have a seat in the den."

The sofa and the four accent chairs covered in chocolate buckskin looked too good to sit on. The legs and arms were deer and elk antlers. The glass coffee table sat on elk antlers, and the side tables next to the chairs were completely wrapped in buffalo skin. There were two large hand-woven baskets on each table. Both filled with fresh eucalyptus and lavender. The accent pieces, the art work, and small knick-knacks around the home were Pomo tribe artifacts.

Dottie felt like she walked back in time.

"I love your comfortable home, Koi. Did you do all the decorating?"

Koi smiled.

"Yes, but I had help. My people started making these things according to tribal rules centuries ago. We just do what we know and appreciate it. I know you feel the same way about your home, right"

Frank interrupted the conversation.

"Would you like a drink, Dottie?

How about you, Tom?"

"I would like a beer, Frank."

"Dottie what about you?"

"Spring water, if you have it."

Koi spoke up.

"We do. We bottled it ourselves from a natural spring on our property."

Tom wanted to know more.

"How much land do you have, Koi?"

"We have 50 acres, but our family owns another 100 acres next to ours. Sherwood Valley Rancheria, which is Pomo reservation sits on another 350 acres."

Tom shook his head and smiled.

"I bet the wildlife enjoys the freedom."

"Yes." Koi liked to talk about her part of the world.

"They are our family too. We still live off the land, so they play an important role in our survival. Frank works at the factory, so we can continue to live like our ancestors lived. My family respects his sacrifice."

Frank came back with drinks and put them in front of his guests. Just as he did, the knocker hit the door plate again.

"More guests. I'll be right back."

Koi kept her seat and kept talking.

"You know the last traditional chief of the Pomo was the great father, Lunkaya."

Tom loved history.

"Was that your grandfather, Koi?"

Koi thought for a moment.

"I think my great-grandfather in your terms. We all have a connection, you know. You and me have a connection, Tom. The Great Spirit, Kuksu, is also my ancestor, we all have that connection. We just call it different names."

Tom loved this kind of conversation. The spirit world

98

always fascinated him, but he never wanted to get too close to it.

Tom just shook his head.

"I always wanted to know what name you called the Great Spirit."

Several more guests entered the den. Tom got up and greeted his fellow workers. Most of them were Pomo tribe members. Max was the only person not in attendance.

Frank followed the guests into the den and looked at Tom.

"Hello Everyone. We have a traditional Pomo meal for you. Please, serve yourself. Some of you might not recognize some of dishes, so we put a card in front of each dish. Dottie and Tom, as our honored guests, you go first."

The couple walked into the dining room and stopped. They looked at the feast. It looked like food at a wedding reception. Fresh salmon, smelt, deer steak, rabbit sausage, squirrel stew, smoked wild mushrooms, an assortment of fresh vegetables, green salad, crushed walnuts, and cashews, sunflower seeds, and an array of cakes filled the dining room table. Tom turned to Dottie as he filled his plate.

"Looks like the only thing missing from this dinner is Max."

Dottie smiled.

99

"I think I saw his shrunken head on the living room mantle, when we walked by."

Tom laughed.

"His head, man, well, way too big to shrink."

Over the course of the dinner Frank told Tom about Max's eccentric habits. Max never interacted with his employees on a personal level. And if anyone left the company, he would never talk to them again. Tom thought that might be the case.

"He's a strange guy, Frank. Why do you work for him? It looks like you don't need him to survive."

"You're right, Tom. I don't need him, but he needs me. We are a holistic people. I mean we look at everyone as if they were a member of our family. Some members cause us a great deal of pain and suffering, but our connection remains. My people respect and honor that connection. Max reminds me of the first white men that invaded our land, and abused it. I work for Max to remind him that this land is ours. His way is not the way of the future. The way of the future is appreciation and respect for all people."

"Man, you bring a whole new meaning to the word liberal. I don't know that I agree with you, but it does sound like the right thing to do for some of us. Me, I do this crazy thing called preservation thinking. But apparently I'm not very good at it. But, I do form my own opinions, and one of them is: do to others what they want to do to you, first."

Dottie listened to conversation and thought about her sisters. Frank brought a whole new thinking process to her world, and she decided she was going to use it.

Part 2

Religion has convinced people that there's an invisible man — living in the sky. Who watches everything you do every minute of every day. And the invisible man has a list of ten specific things he doesn't want you to do. And if you do any of these things, he will send you to a special place, of burning and fire and smoke and torture and anguish for you to live forever, and suffer, and suffer, and burn, and scream, until the end of time. But he loves you and he needs money.

George Carlin

Chapter 8

The reason people use a crucifix against vampires is because vampires are allergic to bullshit.
 Richard Pryor

Tom never used the company membership to the gym when he worked for Deluxe. But his mother's death, and the fact that he was almost forty-two made him rethink his view on longevity. He decided to sign up for a single membership at the Willits local gym even though he didn't fully believe that working out would prolong his life. He didn't want to admit it, but he noticed the impact exercise has on the body when the muscular young man at the front desk processed his application.

"You're going to love it here, Mr. Donovan. My name is Sal Decker. We'll get you feeling good and eating right in eight weeks or less if you follow our routine."

Tom felt the annoyance bug percolating inside of him. The young man's long blonde hair, bulging muscles, and confidence made him question his personal lifestyle.

"Oh, I don't know about that, Sal. Not interested in joining any groups or listening to some drill instructor tell me what to do."

"Don't worry, Tom. May I call you Tom?" Tom nodded his

head. "You can develop your own workout if you want.

We're here to help if you need us. How do you want to pay your membership fee?"

Tom wrote him a check for the first month and then looked around the medium size gym. It looked like every exercise machine known to man was in that gym. And every machine had someone on it. Middle aged men as well as young women worked the treadmills; and young guys climbed the stair climbers. Plus, a group of young men and women pumped iron on the muscle machines. And then he saw an older guy lifting free weights. Tom focused on that guy.

"Who's the guy pumping iron over there, Sal? He looks like he's in great shape."

Sal turned his head and turned back.

"Yeah, that's Jake Ross. He's seventy-five and can lift more weight than most twenty-one-year-olds."

"Seventy-five, Damn" Tom couldn't believe it. Jake was not that big height -wise. Maybe 5'9" or so, but his upper body was in Arnold's league. His well-developed calf muscles, and his six pack keep the gym talking.

"Old Jake's real famous around here, Tom. He's in the gym every other day, and when he's not here he's swimming, running, or biking. He won the AAU title of Mr. America back in the forties, I think. He beat Steve Reeves, the original Hercules, for the title during one competition back then."

Tom watched Jake pump iron. He immediately walked over and introduced himself.

"Mr. Ross, my name is Tom Donovan. Man, where do you get all that energy."

Jake slowly put the 130 lb. bar on the floor and put his hand out.

"Howdy Tom, nice to meet you. You want to know where I get all my energy. I get it the same place you do. We all have it. We just don't use it. The body is a fine-tuned machine. In fact, it is the most perfect machine ever made. The beauty of it is it can be sculptured the way you want. Most folks let their body go to hell as they age, but not me. I believe in the power of the mind. The mind shapes the body. Off course exercise and food are the tools that help the mind work."

Tom listened carefully to Jake. His thoughts seemed right. His mind did some incredible things, when he let it focus on the task at hand.

"Would you consider helping me learn how to lift correctly, Jake? If I'm going to do this, I want to do it right, and it looks like you know what right is."

Jake smiled as he pulled the worn black kidskin gloves off his hands.

105

"Sure, son. But remember we're all amateurs. The difference is some of us are more professional about our amateurism than others. I'll be here the day after tomorrow. We can start then. I like to start around 9, and I usually finish around 12:00."

Tom felt the energy swirl through his body.

"Great. I'll be here at 9. Thanks Jake."

"Don't thank me yet. You might be cursing me before the week is out."

"Nah, I got plenty of other things to curse at, Jake. Forget that that list, sir."

Jake grabbed his gym bag and started walking toward the front door. Tom walked with him. He knew he found a forever friend.

The noisy front door of the B&B kept getting noisier. Tom mumbled as he walked into the parlor. He couldn't wait to tell Dottie about Jake. Dottie and a new guest sat on the sofa drinking tea and talking. Dottie didn't get up, but the guest did.

"Tom, this is Brie Miller. Brie booked this week with us. She lives in Nashville."

Tom smiled.

"My brother lives in Nashville. We love that town. My parents, sorry my dad, lives there too. Do you live on the lake?"

Tom didn't explain his mother's death. He didn't want to think about it.

"No, I live in Bellevue."

"Yes, I know where that is. My brother and dad live in Franklin. What brings you out here, Amy?"

Dottie answered for Brie as Brie sat down.

"Brie is an energy healer. And she plans to take a course at the University of Spiritual Healing on Central Ave."

He looked at Dottie.

"Energy healer? I sort of fit into that category too. I talk to myself because my answers are the only ones I agree with."

Brie laughed, and so did Dottie. Tom continued his monologue before the women could catch a breath.

"I just met an interesting seventy-five-year-old guy who stays in unbelievable shape. He heals himself through exercise, diet, and mind control. I plan to work out with him the day after tomorrow."

Dottie looked at Tom.

"What do you plan to do? Hold his water bottle?"

Brie and Dottie broke up.

"That's real funny, Dot. No. I plan to start lifting weights. He's my body healer, I guess."

Brie felt Tom's sarcasm about her calling, so she jumped into the conversation.

"Hey, anytime we use our mind and focus on what we want as opposed to what we don't want we begin a healing process. I just happen to heal the energy points called Charkas. They are part of our aura.

Dottie knew about Charkas. She loved acupuncture and massages. Before she could add something to the conversation Tom chimed in.

"Oh yeah, Charkas reminds me of that weird religion Carlin talked about."

Brie nodded her head. "What's that, Tom?"

"It's call Frisbeetarianism. It's a religion that claims that when you die, your spirit goes up on your roof, and it gets stuck."

Brie burst into solid laughter, and so did Dottie.

"Anyway, Tom. We are all healers. We all have the ability to heal ourselves. Modern medicine changed our beliefs about healing, so most of us put our faith in medicine instead of the ourselves."

Tom saw an opening.

"I guess all of you health nuts will feel pretty dumb someday lying in your hospital beds and dying of nothing. Be careful what you read in health books. You may die of a misprint."

The girls cracked up. Brie stood up.

"I like that line, Tom. I don't want to die of a misprint."

Dottie started to end the conversation. She got up from the sofa and smiled.

"If you need anything let me know. I'll see you at breakfast around eight tomorrow morning. Is that time still good for you?"

"Yes. I don't have to be in class until 10:00."

When Dottie reached the porch, Tom looked up from the computer.

"I see we have another flake from never-never-land staying with us. There must be a sign posted somewhere on high-way 101 that says all flakes are welcomed at the President Bed and Breakfast in Willits"

"If you want to keep the flakes away, build a website for us?"

"Good idea. I guess the website could be a tool for concealing the truth."

"What truth, Tom?"

"The truth is this place is a conservatively correct, political right, antireligious safe haven that is un-hippie friendly. How does that sound?"

"It sounds like your trip to the gym fried your brain. This is California, Tom, not New England. No witch hunt here. We accept all people regardless of their beliefs."

"I know that's right, Dot. Somehow we manage to attract every nut this side of the Rockies."

"Speaking of nuts; Hazel called. They are coming Friday and will be here all next week."

"Did you tell her the B&B has no bed for her, Dot?"

"No. She is my sister. I want to get through to her somehow. Maybe Brie can clear her Charkas while she's here? Maybe she could work on Eddie, Lois, and Todd too?"

"Well, that's one way to make sure Brie never comes back. I like the way you think, Dot. You still have the normal girl mind I married."

"Tom, just work on the website, and let me handle the guests. Normal is nothing more than a computersetting on a new washing machine."

Tom laughed. Dottie did too, and then she touched Tom on the shoulder.

"Are you serious about working out?"

"I need to do something. My computer business is slow, and I need to get rid of some of this stress. I miss the dogs."

"I know Tom. I miss them too, but you know."

Tom had tears in his eyes.

"Let's go look at those two Bulldog puppies tomorrow."

He heard the dogs' voice again. "We like this part. Happiness always follows us in puppy stage."

Dottie smiled.

"You know at times you make a lot of sense. Maybe your exercise program will increase your make-sense meter."

Tom looked at the computer screen, and then he smiled at Dottie.

"Maybe so, Dot. You know what Leno said about that don't you?"

Dottie knew a Tomism was on the way.

"Oh here we go. What did he say?"

"He said: Give a man a fish and he will eat for a day. Teach a man to fish and he will eat for a lifetime. Teach a man to create an artificial shortage of fish, and he will eat steak."

"Really Tom. No clue what that means, and I don't think you do either."

Tom smiled and stood up.

"Dot you forgot something—there's no turn-off switch when I'm in genius mode."

Chapter 9

In reality, all men are sculptors, constantly chipping away the unwanted parts of their lives trying to create a masterpiece.

Eddie Murphy

It didn't take long for Jake to turn Tom into a mass of muscle. Tom's 5'8" stocky frame looked stocky, but the weight lifting really made him look like a sculptured rock. Tom got addicted to the workouts. He continued to pump iron with Jake for seven years, and even got his friend, Jack Doyle interested in body conditioning. One day after the three men finished a grueling power-lifting session Jack walked out of the gym with Tom.

"Are we on some kind of ego trip, Tom? I mean, what's so important about having the biggest muscles in town?"

Jack didn't connect with the workout routine. He had other things to do. He had a business to run, and his wife and daughter wanted him to stop getting so buff. That's what Riley called it. Jackie liked the new dad, but Riley told him he was getting too old to have big muscles.

"Come on now, Jack. Look at Jake. It's not about ego with him. It's a way of life."

Jack frowned at Tom.

113

"He's a muscle building addict, Tom. That's all he thinks about. I don't mind working out a couple of times a month, not a couple of times a day."

"What's the matter, Jack? You gotta believe in your talent, not your flaws. Manage your talents and you manage your life better. Ever since I got in shape, the number of nut jobs we book at the B&B went down considerably. I even picked up three new computer clients. Plus, the city hired me to redo all their computer programs. Jake played a role in getting me that job. He introduced me to the city manager. It seems like the more muscle I get, the more money I make."

Jack shook his head in disbelief.

"You think all that is workout related, Tom? Are you serious?"

"You bet I am. Why just last week we had a state senator staying with us. He brought his Hollywood actress girlfriend with him. They stayed for a week and paid top dollar."

"I heard about that. Dottie told Barbie that Senator Gumas and his secret squeeze were in the house. You know that actress is his mistress, don't you?"

"Yeah, I know, but at least they were quiet when they were having sex. And they didn't play kissy face at the breakfast table. Plus, I agree with some of Bill's political ideas. He wants to get rid of these freeloaders that waste our tax money."

"Are you talking about the rise in illegal immigrants in California?"

"You bet I am. I'm sick of people not taking responsibility for their actions, Jack."

Jack thought for a minute.

I think Letterman made a point the other night on that subject."

Tom knew it was game on.

"I don't watch him that much anymore. What did he say?"

Jack looked up at the sky, and then he smiled at Tom.

"He said: there are about 12 million illegal immigrants in this country. But if you ask a Native American, that number is more like 300 million."

Tom laughed.

"He's right about that. We are all ignorant immigrants in one way or another. But Gumas thinks these illegal sombreros take jobs away from US citizens and should be sent home. I agree with him."

"Really Tom? When's the last time you saw a taxpaying citizen doing manual labor? We all want to be managers and bosses. We want our kids to be college graduates who excel in everything, but manual labor. Our middle class wants to live the American dream, and let someone else do the hard work. Gumas forgets that we need low paid workers to do the hard work for us. And the only folks who will do that sort of work are from third world nations. To them working for a respectable hourly wage is the American dream."

Tom got serious.

"They have to pay to live that American dream by getting into this country the right way."

"And what is the right way, Tom? Do you have any idea how much paperwork, money, and time it takes to get a work visa? Our laws let only the rich and connected crooks get into the country the right way. You got to know someone or pay someone to live the American dream, if you're not American, Tom. You know that."

Tom didn't give in.

"I believe in the right way not the wrong way. I think Gumas got a handle on the right way."

"The only thing he's got a handle on is that actress. He wants to influence conservatives like you— that look the other way when it comes to ethics."

"Now wait a minute, Jack. Never underestimate the power of dumb people in huge groups. Gumas wants to send those groups back to their roots. That's all."

Are you saying Senator Bill Gumas is not a nutcase? He's as nutty as a fruit cake. He is one of those Republicans, Tom!"

Tom smiled. He loved to argue with Jack. They were different politically, but they did share the same value system.

Jack started to laugh as he spoke.

"You know Tom the only criminal class in this country sits up there in Washington. Just when I think I know what and where my tax dollars go, they change the plan. They conditioned us to believe bullshit only comes from certain places. I'm here to tell you bullshit is everywhere, and you conservatives are up to your necks in it."

Tom enjoyed a good laugh, and Jack made him laugh.

"Honestly, Tom if the good lord wanted us to put our faith in guys like that, he would make honest candidates."

Both men reached their cars, shook hands, and smiled. Tom continued to chuckle as Jack jumped in his car. Both men knew it was okay to agree to disagree. Tom just wanted to have the last word.

"We'll continue this conversation on Friday, buddy. That will give you time to think about this great opportunity we are experiencing."

Jack looked puzzled as he started the car.

"Anytime you call me buddy, Tom I know I'm in trouble. I wouldn't call sore muscles and crap from the family a great opportunity."

"I'll talk to Barbie and the kids, Jack. You know they will listen to me."

Jack grabbed the door handle and looked at Tom.

"Don't do me anymore favors, Tom. You got me into this mess, and I have to get myself out of it."

"It's not a mess, Jack. It's exercise!"

"You know what Riley calls it Tom? She calls it Tomersize."

Jack pulled the door closed and put the car in drive. Tom stood there shaking his head for a second. He knew Jack would come around. He always did. Dottie liked to call them the Ying and Yang of Willits. Tom did really know what she meant by that, but he had a pretty good idea. Tom walked over to his red mustang convertible and got in. He suddenly thought about what he said to the girls when the dogs and his mother died a few years back. As he started the car, he mumbled to himself.

"You might be a Mustang to everyone else, but you're a Mastiff to me."

The dogs'voice was front and center. "We always liked that line, Tom.

The type of guests staying at the B&B seemed to change as the decade changed. Tom didn't know it at the time, but his beliefs about people constantly change, and he attracted different type of experiences thanks to his workout regime and attitude. The computer business was in growth mode. And his stature in town seemed to be on the rise. He was a solid citizen. For the past two years, he even stayed at his lawyer-client, Bill Backland's condo on Maui, when family vacation time rolled around.

Backland specialized in family law issues. Tom wasn't sure what he really did because the information he programed didn't always reflect family law issues. He asked Bill that question while picking up the keys to the condo for the upcoming trip.

"Bill, I know your sign says family law, but what does that mean? I notice you handle divorces, wills, and stuff like that, but some of the clients I see in your records no marriage or will documentation. Some of these clients have stores, but the stores don't show any sales. How do they stay in business?"

Bill sat behind a large oak desk in his small office. He wore a Tommy Bahama shirt and a pair of TB Khaki shorts. His long brown hair parted on the left. The horn rim glasses covered most of his rosacea covered face, so he looked like a forty-year-old cartoon character instead of a lawyer. As Tom asked him that famous question, Bill started to light a cigar.

"You want a cigar, Tom?"

"No man, my father use to smoke those nasty things. My hair smelled like cigar smoke when I went to school. I took a verbal beating over that and a few other personal things when I was in younger skin."

"So how did you handle the razzing?"

"It was easy, Bill; I rebelled. I might look like a mild mannered guy who follows the team. But, I tell people there's no "I" in team. But there is an "I" in integrity independence, and individuality."

Bill laughed and then took a puff on his cigar. Tom got up, and walked to the small window. The smoke annoyed him.

"So what's going on with these stores, Bill? Are they fronts for another business?"

Tom had a pretty good idea what these store owners were doing, but he wanted his friend Bill to confirm his suspicions.

"Right. Sorry Tom. By the way, I do handle all the stuff you mentioned and a few more issues. The other issues involve an illegal substance. I know you won't say a word to anyone.

120

Bill put his cigar in the ashtray and opened the top drawer of his desk. He pulled out a folder.

"Take a look at this, and tell me you wouldn't do the same thing?"

Tom opened the folder and saw a ledger. There were multiple large dollar number entries.

Tom heard the dogs again. "When we got a bone, we buried it. We didn't smoke it."

"That's the kind of money they pay me to make them look legit. That's how I bought the condo in Maui. You know something Tom? At least fifty million Americans smoked marijuana at some point in their lives. And the only folks who didn't like it were, Bill Clinton, Clarence Thomas, and Judge Ginsberg."

Tom laughed. "I always wondered why recreational drugs don't come in suppository form."

Bill liked that and laughed.

"They say honesty is the best policy, Bill. But apparently the law eliminated that, and made dishonesty the second-best policy."

Bill gave Tom a strange smirky look and changed the subject.

"Oh, you need the keys, right?"

Bill opened a lower drawer on the right side of the desk.

"Here ya go, Pal. Enjoy your stay. Dee Dee and I just got back. The weather was a ten, and the girls loved it. Are all the girls going?"

Tom wanted to continue the conversation.

"Yes the girls and even Tiffany are on the Hawaiian travel list. We all love it over there, but that 'aloha' stuff can play with your head. The islanders say it when I meet them and they say when I leave them. I guess it proves too much sun fries the brain.

They don't know the difference between hello and goodbye."

Bill laughed again.

"Daughter Betsy told me Tiffany had some sort of run in with one of the girls before graduation. Did you know about that back then, Tom?"

"Well, Tiffany was Valedictorian as well as president of her High school class. All of her classmates liked her except Penny Green. Penny came to the senior prom drunk and confronted Tiffany. Penny called Tiffany gay in front of Tiffany's boyfriend and several girlfriends."

"Oh boy. The Greens have a lot of money. I guess you let that one slide. Tom, you did let it slide, right?"

"Hell no, man. I took care of that situation fast."

"Oh yeah? How did you do that big guy?"

Bill liked to call Tom big guy.

"We invited Penny and her parents, over to the B&B and we had a meeting. Her dad was a no show. When Penny and her mother came into the parlor, I knew it was game on. The mother smiled and Penny frowned. The first thing the mom said was 'let's not lose our state of nirvana. Let's hold hands and be kind to each other."

Bill smiled. He couldn't wait to hear what was next.

"What did you say, big guy?"

"I told her no hand-holding nonsense. And I also told her I did not know about nirvana, but I visited Idaho once. Then I said if you don't get control of your daughter's mouth I will. Penny started to shake, and she started crying. Dottie and Tiffany just sat there. They didn't know what to say."

"Ah, I bet her mother didn't like that, did she?"

"I really didn't care. She got up and grabbed Penny's hand, and they both left in a hurry. I don't think Penny sees Tiffany anymore. I think she moved to one of the Southern states. Justice served, my friend."

Chapter 10

Anything you have to acquire a taste for was not meant to be eaten.

Eddie Murphy

Any visit from Hazel and Todd and their kids was a miserable experience for Tom. Dottie handled the visits better, but she usually got annoyed at some point during their stay. Her time with her sister was a little more manageable. Hazel's kids were older and didn't want to make the 2 ½ hour car ride from Palo Alto to Willits. Hazel was not aging gracefully, even though she had everything she always wanted.

Hazel sat in the parlor with Dottie one Friday night in May. The Glendale train crash still fresh in Hazel's mind. One of her sorority sister's was on one of the trains that derailed when it hit an abandoned SUV left on the tracks. Her friend, Patsy Close was one of the eleven people killed in that incident.

"I still can't believe Patsy was on one of those trains, Dottie. You remember her, right? She was my best friend all through school. She had it all— money, power, beauty, charm, and brains. I can't figure out why she travelled by train. Her husband, Don, bought her two cars. She must

Be up to something crazy. Maybe she had a secret lover."

Just as she finished, Tom walked in with Brando and Dante.

"Are you finally telling your sister about your secret love life, Hazel?"

Dottie jumped in.

"Okay, Tom. Hazel was talking about her friend, Patsy."

Tom took a seat in the rocker and the two dogs found a comfortable spot in front of Dottie.

"I'm joking Hazel. I know you madly love Todd. By the way, where is that Silicon Valley sailor?"

Hazel didn't smile. Tom hit a nerve, and he knew he did.

"Todd needed a massage. He's a little stressed. Lois dates a boy ten years older. He's a black biker from Oakland."

Dottie wasn't surprised. Lois and Eddie were always out of control looking for some sort of wild adventure. Dottie wasn't sure what to say, but she opened her mouth and heard words come out.

"Did you meet him? Where did she meet him?"

Hazel wanted sympathy, but she knew she knew none was on the way from Tom, so she turned to Dottie.

"On line and no, we don't know him. We just pray that it's nothing serious. We know Jesus will protect her from this dead beat."

Tom found his opening. He couldn't past this opportunity. His annoyance with Hazel became obvious once again.

"You know the old saying: if you have to acquire a taste for somebody they might end of being your best friend."

Hazel looked at Tom. Her eyes looked and felt like daggers.

"What the hell is that supposed to mean? I don't have to acquire a taste for anything. I never eat broccoli for that very reason."

Tom shook his head affirmatively.

"Broccoli and bikers. That's what it sounds like to me."

Hazel asked Dottie to get her a glass of wine, and then she looked at Tom.

"Jesus will take care of this. That's the taste I need."

"Really Hazel? I would never want to be part of a group that worshipped a man nailed to two pieces of pine."

Tom didn't give in.

"*I* don't think Jesus has anything to do with Lois and her relationship, Hazel. What makes you think this guy is a deadbeat?

I know lots of black guys that ride bikes and none of them are dead beats. They just like Harley's. I talk to them all the time at the gym."

Hazel wasn't going to let his comment pass. Jesus was her savior, and the bible was her salvation. White women and black men aren't mentioned as love partners in the bible, so in her mind Lois qualifies as a sinner.

"You are hypocrite, Tom. Our daughter lives in a state of sin, and I think you are too. God will make sure you both pay for that. We can only pray he shows mercy."

Dottie came back with the wine. She wanted to add something, but Tom cut her off.

"You really don't believe all that crap. Do you, Hazel?"

"Crap? It's the word of God. I hope your opinions don't rub off on your girls. That's all I can say."

"Okay you two. Let's stop right there before this gets uglier. Hazel, you can believe what you want to believe. Tom has that freedom as well. Maybe Lois needs help identifying the consequences for questionable choices. We live what we think, and it sounds like Lois thinks she knows what's up."

"And what that might be, Dot?" Hazel didn't understand where Dottie was going with that comment, but Tom did, so he spoke up.

"She wants to piss you and Todd off. She wants to prove to you that she has the ability to make her own decisions without your help."

"I don't remember you going to school for a degree in psychology, Tom. We will handle Lois in our own way, and that means God will be our guide, not your beliefs. I don't want to talk about this anymore."

Hazel got up and went upstairs. Dottie and the dogs immediately went out the front door without saying a word. Tom sat there wondering how Hazel could be so narrow minded. He knew, right? As he sat there, he remembered a Lenny Bruce line. Lenny talked about Catholics and their bigoted opinions about righteousness. Lenny told the audience:

"If Jesus died sixty years ago, Catholic school children would be wearing little electric chairs around their necks instead of crosses."

The dogs' voice was back. "See we told you all that heaven and hell stuff is religious stuff. All religions prepare for war, are at war, or recovering from a war. They think they have to fight for right, but there is no right here, right?"

Tom started to laugh out loud. Then he heard Lenny's voice in his head again:

"The only honest art form is comedy. You can't fake it—try to fake three laughs in an hour; they'll take you away, man. You can't."

Lenny thought. comedy was an art form and an honest one. Comedians make truths—untruths. His mind clicked to Leno's Friday night monologue: *You can't stay mad at someone who makes you laugh.* Tom thoughts turned to his conversation with Hazel. He realized he shouldn't stay mad at Hazel. She can be a great comedian, because she deeply believes in her own righteousness.

Brick and Dena Morgan lived in one of the 1930s bungalows across the street from the B&B. The couple didn't have kids. It was the second marriage for both of them. Tom didn't meet the couple in 2002, when they first moved into the old house. That old home was a disaster. It took Brick and Dena six months to turn the home into an art deco showplace. Tom saw Brick one Saturday morning watering his small, beautiful new rose garden. He immediately called out to his new neighbor.

"Hi neighbor! Welcome to the neighborhood. I'm Tom Donovan."

Brick turned off the hose and went to the end of his lot line.

"Nice place you got there, Tom. I'm Brick Morgan."

Tom walked over to Brick.

"Sorry I didn't introduce myself before now, but I didn't want to disturb your remodeling project. Did you guys move here from another state?"

Brick took his rubber gloves off and looked at Tom.

"I grew up in Santa Rosa, and my wife's from Northridge."

Tom turned his head and Brick did too. They looked up the quiet California sycamore lined street and saw another neighbor's dog running wild.

"I wish people would keep their dogs where they belong. We have two trained dogs, thanks to my wife Dottie. But tell me more. Why did you move up here?"

The dogs came back in Carlin's voice. "This scene reminds us that a dog can express more in minutes wagging his tail than a man can after talking for hours."

Brick had some time and loved to talk.

"Well, my wife Dena is a singer and musician. She grew up in Northridge, California. Her parents performed in Vegas in Wayne Newton's show nine months a year, so she had a taste of the fast life in her early years. Her 5'9" frame, natural blonde hair, and deep set blue eyes complimented her personality. She wanted to become a beautiful showgirl, and thanks to her parents' connections in Vegas she fulfilled that dream. Dena had the gift of grab, a great body, and a singing voice that sounds a little like Cher, so she was one of the regulars at the Stardust. She married a musician when she was twenty-one, but that marriage ended when she found her husband in bed with male member of his rock group. She was thirty when she made that discovery. She vowed never to marry again. She decided to get away from Vegas, so she moved to Santa Rosa to sing in the Marriot lounge and start a new life. Santa Rosa feels like. Her dad grew up there."

Tom smiled and wiped his forehead with the back of his hand.

"Wow! It's going to be a hot one today. I can't wait to meet her. Is she working now?"

"Yes, she is a dance instructor at the Fred Murray, I mean Arthur Murray Dance studio."

Tom smiled and grabbed Brick's arm.

"Maybe I should start taking dance lessons, so I'm ready when the girls get married. How did you two meet?"

"That's another good story. I grew up in Santa Rosa too. When I turned eighteen, I decided to join the marines. My parents wanted me to go to USC, but school was not for me. I wanted to see the world and experience life outside of Northern California. My parents couldn't understand why a lanky 6'1" pacifist like me would want to go to war and the marines didn't either. When I went for my interview, the big marine sergeant got side-tracked by my travel agenda. He started the conversation something like this:

"So you want to join the marines. You do want to fight, Mr. Morgan?"

"I had a blank look on my face, but I managed to say, heck no! I'm against killing. I just want to travel, and I thought joining the marines would help me achieve that goal."

"The sergeant knew kids like me who have no business in that branch of the service so he said:"

"I think you should consider the Peace Corps, son. That group might be a better fit. Marines train to fight and protect. Marines don't travel for fun."

"I looked uncomfortable, but I wasn't. I felt relieved in one way. Then I said the first thing that popped into my mind."

"I'm not interested in seeing Africa or places where there's a lot of poverty and suffering, sir. I want to see Paris, London, Rome, and maybe Athens. You know what I mean. I want a worldly education."

"I could tell he was a little annoyed, but he politely said:"

"You might want to go to Vegas, son. I heard some of those casinos are made to look like some of those places. That's the only advice I have for you today. Thanks for coming in."

"I really woke up after that meeting. I got the marines out of my mind. I had enough money saved, so I went to Vegas for the first time. I stayed at the Stardust for $29 a night, and saw the Paris-inspired topless show called the "Lido Revue." I didn't realize it then, but my future wife was on stage flaunting her assets. After my Vegas trip, I found my calling as an assistant repairman for an apartment complex in Santa Rosa. Funny enough, London Place Apartments was the name of the large complex. I worked there for over ten years, and I learned how to fix just about everything. In the late 1996, the apartment complex sold to an investment group in LA, and they replace the staff with their own hand-picked employees. I was out of a job, so I moved out of my apartment.

I knew I could find full-time work around town, and I did. I saw an ad in the local paper for a handyman at the Marriot, Santa Rosa. I applied, and got the job. I worked there for two years, but never went into the lounge. I worked days and was on call at night. One night, I got a call from the bartender about a water leak under the bar. I immediately knew what to do. I went to main water turn-off point in the utility room and then went to the lounge to correct the issue. That's when my life changed forever.
Dena's voice hit me like a ton of brinks. I couldn't take my eyes off of her."

Tom thought about the story for a minute, and then he started to chuckle.

"Did you fix the leak or did you just stand there and drool?"

"I drooled while fixing it."

"That's a great story, Brick. How did you get together? Did you ask her out after she finished the song?"

"No, I went to the lounge every night and stayed until she stopped singing. One night she came over to my table after her set and asked me if I could fix her toilet. I didn't think she noticed me. I flipped-out, so I had a hard time answering her."

Tom thought for a moment. The idea Brick didn't say anything was hard to imagine given the current conversation.

"So what did you finally say or do?"

"Well, I shook my head and asked her where she lived. And do you know what, Tom?"

"No, what?"

"She lived in my new apartment complex, The Roman Terrace. She was in B building, and I was in the A building."

"Didn't the apartment have a handyman?"

"Yeah, it was me. I worked for them part-time. She knew who I was long before I knew her."

Tom nodded his head in agreement.

"I guess I know the rest of the story. You fell in love, got married, and moved here."

"We did fall in love, and we did move here, but we didn't

get married the typical way."

Tom knew another load of life was ready to drop, and he wanted to hear it.

"Typical? I don't think there is a typical, Brick. If you're in love and committed, you're married as far as I'm concerned. Some preacher with a white collar and a black robe holding an elaborate ritual has nothing to do with the union of two people. I belonged to the Catholic Church until I realized limbo was a Caribbean dance."

Brick smiled.

"Man, I like the way you think. We feel the same way, so we asked a friend to read our hand-written vows at the Santa Rosa airport."

"Oh, did you fly somewhere for a honeymoon after that?"

"No, we just had the ceremony there. We're both a fly phobia, so we rented a car a drove up here. We knew we had to move here after spending seven days sightseeing."

"That's a great story, Brick. Do you do any painting?"

"Painting? Do you mean house painting or canvas artwork?"

Tom pointed to the front of the B&B.

"House painting. We need to get a couple of coats of paint on the outside of this beauty, and I thought you might be interested. We can't pay a lot, but we might be able to trade
135

with you."

"Sure Tom. We'll work something out. I can't wait to tell Dena about you."

Tom turned and started to walk away, and as he did, he smiled at Brick.

"You don't know that much about me, Brick. You did all the talking."

Brick shook his head up and down.

"Yeah, right. But, we heard all about you guys from the neighbors next door. Walt Sensinger likes to talk, Tom."

"Walt's a great guy, but you can't believe all you hear, my friend. The advice I like to give is don't take anyone's advice, especially when it comes to people. Come over later and I'll tell you the real story. It's always better to get the scoop first hand. We do have a couple of guests tonight, but they went to the coast, so they won't be back until later this evening. Please, I want to meet your wife. We'll have some pasta with my special gravy"

"Are you sure? Maybe you should check with your wife, first. I've got to talk to Dena too."

"I'm sure you guys are what Dottie needs. She's looking for a spark of down-to-earth honesty. And I think you guys can turn that spark into a flame of friendship."

"Thank you, Tom. That's really neighborly of you."

Chapter 11

The Statue of Liberty is no longer saying, "Give me your poor, your tired, your huddled masses." She's got a base-ball bat and yelling, "You want a piece of me?"

Tomin Williams

"I must tell you, Tom; that's the best tomato sauce I ever tasted. I'd love the recipe."

Dena put her fork down, and picked up the white linen napkin on her lap. She liked the Donovan's and the way they lived. When Brick told her about the dinner invitation, she had trepidations. Neighbor Walt Sensinger told them about Tom's short fuse and difficult personality. Walt described Tom as an East coast redneck who was rough around the edges. He described Dottie as an energetic nut-job that loved animals more than people. Dena didn't see them that way, but she wanted to confirm what she believed.

Tom finished the last bit of chicken on his plate. He took a drink of his special juice, and wiped his mouth with the back of his hand.

Dottie watched that old habit and couldn't resist.

"Use your napkin, Tom. We're not in Philly anymore."

Tom looked at her and the Morgan's.

"Please excuse my bad manners. I have an impersonal trainer who encourages my bad habits."

Dena and Brick laughed. Dena spoke first.

"We do too, Tom. Tell us more about the sauce."

Tom felt relieved. His roots showed, but they seem welcomed by these new friends. He picked up his glass, brought it to his lips, and then put it down without drinking. He smiled at Dena.

"The tomato, as a food plant, originated in Mexico and spread around the world after the Spanish colonized America. There are 7,500 different varieties of tomatoes. Italy didn't start using them as food until 1548. England didn't start growing them until 1890. I started growing tomatoes several years ago. I usually plant over thirty plants each year, and they are all different varieties. I grow the Plum, Heirloom, Campari, Grape, Cherry, Beefsteak, Ox heart, and Pear varieties. I use all of them to make my gravy, but the Plum and the Heirloom seem to have the best flavor. That's my opinion of course. The rest of my recipe is top secret."

Tom hesitated and looked at his wife.

"Even Dottie doesn't have a clue."

Dottie looked at her husband and then at Dena.

"It's not like I'm dying to know, Dena. I make a pretty decent tomato sauce too. I use the Campari because of the sweetness, and the Pear because they produce a gourmet taste. We offer gourmet meals to our guest. Breakfast is our specialty."

Dena changed the subject. She heard all she needed to hear about tomatoes. She liked to cook, but she didn't get that excited about it.

"How long have you known Walt and Millie Sensinger?"

Dena addressed Dottie. She wanted to see if Tom would jump in, or let his wife answer the question.

"Oh, about four years I guess. Millie helps me clean the B&B sometimes, and Walt helped Tom build the pond in the side yard a couple of years ago. I think the two of them had a difficult time with each other. It was right after the Twin Towers went down, so opinions got in the way of some of the work. Millie is a sweetheart. She never says a harsh word about anybody or anything. I don't know much more about Walt except what Tom told me."

Brick nursed a glass of red wine and listened. He didn't like to talk about people, so he didn't interrupt.

"What about Walt, Tom. I like to know if I've got a wacko living next door."

Tom knew he had to be careful. Brick suddenly got interested in the conversation.

"Walt's a great guy and a good neighbor. No worries there, Dena. Walt likes to talk. That's his job. He's the news guy on the local AM radio station. His ideas about political and social issues that impact my family don't line up with mine, but that's life I guess."

Brick perked up.

"What kind of issues, Tom. I hope you don't mind me asking. I'm on the conservative side and I think you might be too.

Tom took a drink of his pomegranate juice.

"I don't meet too many native Californians that think like me, Brick. Walt is a pacifist, gay rights advocate, save the planet promoter and an illegal alien proponent. I guess I should accept all those things, but I don't because most folks don't get it, you know what I mean? The United States is the only country where IQ's and the life longevity recently passed each other in the opposite directions."

Brick and Dena cracked up. Dottie was not amused. She was old school about social conversations. Topics like politics and religion are not meant to be dinner topics.

The dogs were back. "Now you know why man's best friend can't talk."

"Okay Tom, let's not bash Walt because of his beliefs. If it was up to you the Statue of Liberty would be holding a "Do Not Enter" sign. I think we all have a right to experience

140

our desires in whatever way we want. That's the principle this country sits on. Gays have a right to marry, and people who want to live in America have a right to experience it. It's not their fault that our laws restrict rather than allow progressive attitudes."

Dena looked at Dottie.

"Yeah, that's right."

Tom knew he had to stop, but once he got started it was hard for him to give in.

"I don't know, Dottie. I think this California air has caused some brain damage."

"I'm glad you realize your flaws, Tom."

Dena and Brick laughed, and so did Tom. It was time to stop and move on. Tom put his napkin on the table and started to get up.

"Let's go sit in the parlor."

Brick got up and followed Tom. He found what he needed to find at that dinner. Tom was an opinionated guy. He stood up for what he believed in. He didn't try to change anyone's opinion; he just expressed his. Brick liked that. He liked Dottie too. Dena didn't agree with everything Tom said, but she did agree that the California air does cause serious brain damage in some folks. That seemed better than saying the pot she needed to sleep at night was harmful to her mental health.

Dena picked up Brick's plate and wine glass and went to the kitchen with Dottie.

"I'm glad we had this time together, Dottie. I enjoyed it. I hope you two will let us reciprocate."

Dottie started putting dishes in the dishwasher.

"Off course, Dena. I want to hear more about you and your dance career."

The rest of the night gave the two couples time to get to know more about each other. The Morgan's even bonded with the bulldogs.

Early the next morning Walt Sensinger stood in his front yard. His attention fixed on a Donovan house guest acting strangely on the front lawn. The guest appeared to be in his late thirties or early forties. His black horn-rimmed glasses and disheveled curly grey and black hair made his Asian features look longer than a normal face. He wore tight black and yellow stretch leotards, and a green and black tank top. His slender body had no muscle definition. His bare feet were three feet apart, and his knees were in the bent position. His arms were at 90 degree angles, and his hands were cutting the air in front of him. His movements were slow and precise. The guest showed no emotion as his legs and arms moved from one position to another. Walt watched the guy for twenty minutes, and finally crossed the narrow street between his house and the Donovan's front lawn. He stopped ten feet away from the guest. While he crossed the street, Tom came out the front door.

Tom heard Walt's question but couldn't see him.

"Excuse me, sir. I don't want to bother you, but is that a form of Tai Chi?"

Walt's sister told him about the ancient Chinese art, but he never saw anyone doing it in Willits. The guest didn't acknowledge Walt's presence. Walt stood there for another ten minutes as the stranger moved the air around him with his hands. When the man completed his workout, he closed his eyes, put his hands together in front of him and took a deep bow. When he opened his eyes, he looked at Walt. Tom continued to watch from the front porch as his guest started to speak.

"Sorry sir for my bad manners, but when I move Chi I don't know what's going on around me. My name is James Chen."

Chen extended his right hand and Walt did the same.

"Nice to meet you, James. Did you say you move Chi?"

"Right. Chi is what Eastern culture calls energy. Air is full of energy, right?"

Walt didn't think about the air that way. Air was air to him.

143

"I guess the air does have energy in it doesn't it?"

Tom mumbled something as he stood on the porch, but he didn't intervene in the conversation.

"Energy is in everything and everybody. We move energy with mind. I put myself in the place where energy comes in my body and stays."

Tom couldn't stand it. He had to jump into the conversation. Once again he had another guest that should be at the psycho-ward, not his B&B.

"Hold on a minute." Walt spotted Tom for the first time when he heard those words.

"You're not serious are you, James? Don't you think that's peculiar and rather archaic behavior?"

Tom wanted a pragmatic explanation.

James had a strange look on his face, and then he began to smile.

"Oh, I just do what my Chinese ancestors do for thousands of years. This kind of movement is everyday exercise for me just like running is for you. If you have to ask what I do, then you don't understand what it is like to move your mind to another place."

Walt looked at Tom, and then he smiled at James.

"I guess he has a point, Tom. I believe the universe and everything in is one big ball of energy. It's like one of those nesting dolls or like peeling an onion. The onion is still the onion when peeled, and the doll is still the doll. They just have different layers, and so does the universe. The only difference is we can never peel all the layers off the universe. Somehow James here, peels layers of his mind, and moves completely out of reality and winds up somewhere else."

Tom started to shake his head as he turned and walked to-ward the front door.

"You really believe that, Walt? Be careful what you read and see especially when it comes to science and health. A misunderstanding might cause death."

Walt didn't want Tom to leave.

"Hey, I know what it's like to be out of it. I had to put my mother in an assisted living home last year because her dementia got worse. Do you know what she did when she settled into that place?"

Tom didn't know what to say. Walt was as strange as James in his mind. Tom looked at Walt as he started to tell his story. He noticed Walt's large pointed nose and Ray Ban sunglasses. The glasses overwhelmed his other facial features. His five-foot eight-inch frame held about 220lbs of fat and flabby muscle. Every time Tom saw Walt he had on a pair of jean shorts with a black deadhead tee shirt. He wore his long gray hair and beard well-groomed like his idol, Jerry Garcia. But the one thing that really stood out about Walt was his radio voice. He used it on and off the air.

James didn't know what to say to the men, so he just shook his head from left to right as Walt continued his story.

"Well, I tell what she did. She found a boyfriend in that place."

James smiled.

"That's good, right?"

"Well when my father found out, and he didn't like it. He said her senility was really stupidity. I guess it's hard to tell the difference sometimes. I had to put him in assisted living last month. I found another place for him in Ukiah. I didn't want him to get between mom and her boyfriend. That's not cool, right?"

Tom forgot about James for a minute, and got interested in Walt's tale.

"Do you mean your mother completely forgot she was married to your father?"

"She sure did. I can't say I blame her. Dad was a pretty controlling and verbally abusive guy through the years, so he got the flower he planted, I guess."

Tom tried to hold back the laughter but couldn't.

"That's a good one, Walt. Do you think your dad will find a girlfriend in that home in Ukiah? That would really be special for sure."

Walt didn't like that thought, so he changed the subject.

"What are you doing in Willits, James?"

James grinned at Tom and then turned to Walt.

"I am professor of ancient civilizations. I give lecture at Mendocino State on Pomo Indians tomorrow. You know Pomo, right?"

Walt shook his head and Tom answered.

"I have a friend who is from the Pomo tribe. What is your talk about, James?"

James walked over to the porch, and sat down on the step in front of Tom. Walt followed him.

"I wrote paper on the connection between Pomo culture and Chinese culture. My research shows that Pomo had Chinese ancestors."

Tom thought for a minute. He assumed the Pomo were from Mexico originally, but he had no proof of that. He looked down at James.

"Interesting idea, James. I guess life is made of facts and happenings, which blow through the mind like storms. Do you have proof the Chinese came to this country before

Columbus?"

James stood up. He liked this kind of conversation even though, at times, his English lacked the necessary words to get his point across.

"Ah, many cultures got here before your Columbus. You make history the way you want not the way it is. Chinese people traveled by water over 10,000 years ago and they found this place. Native people were already here then. They came from Mexico and some Pacific islands. These people had sex together and made another tribe, another language, and another reality. People do that sort of thing for many centuries. We do it now. Just look around you. You see black with white, White with Asia people, black with Asia people, Indian with Chinese, and they all have babies. Every one changing looks, and way they think. We constantly change DNA in order to grow as a species."

Walt shook his head affirmatively.

"Makes sense to me, James. How did you figure all this out?"

"Many years' study at university in Shanghai. We have old records. You don't know about."

Tom jumped in once again.

"I always say never let school get in the way of education, James. I don't want to spend the rest of my life worrying about things that never happened. I experienced a lot of terrible things in my life, and some of them actually happened."

Walt and James laughed. James started to walk up the steps. He touched Tom on the shoulder as he passed him.

"Okay, I know. You rather keep a foolish thought than hear my knowledge because you like to believe knowledge the foolish way, right?"

Tom laughed, and so did Walt. Tom believed his thoughts rocked. He did have a head of stone at times. His girls knew it, and his friends saw it, and accepted it. He knew a laugh went a long way when stubbornness ruled.

"Remember James. Be thankful for the fools. We make the rest of you look good."

James went inside. Walt started to walk away, but he had to say something, so he stopped and turned toward Tom.

"That guy does make some sense, Tom. We change all the time. Who really knows what happened 10 or 20 centuries ago let alone 100 centuries ago. We do make our history. Old James here showed us that we don't know what we think we know. He knows more about us than we know about him."

Tom smiled.

"Yeah, why is it that we call everyone else's stuff, shit, and we call our shit, stuff. It's kind of the same thing with history ain't it?"

Chapter 12

Get your facts first, and then you can distort
them as much as you please.
Mark Twain

When Tom's dad came to visit in October, 2003 he didn't know what to expect. Seven years passed, but his mom's death was still fresh in his mind. His 82-year-old father, John Tom, brought his 67-year-old live-in girlfriend with him. Her first name was the same as his mother's. John Tom liked to call them Peggy 1 and Peggy 2. Peggy 2 was Peggy Pickens a Nashville native. John Tom's grief was in high gear while Peggy 1 was in hospice care. Peggy 2 lived in an adjacent apartment. She cared for her eighty-five-year-old mother. She survived two husbands, and looked for a third every chance she got. She brought John Tom baked goods and meals, and when Peggy 1 passed, she moved in with him.

When the couple pulled up and parked in front of the B&B, Tom's nerves hit the wall. He never spent any time around this woman, and he didn't know what to expect.

"Showtime, Dottie. Let's both go to the door. I need your support. I think insanity finally invaded my family."

Dottie smiled.

"Well then. I can't wait to meet her. Pay back is hell."

The couple walked up the front steps to the opened front door, and as they did they noticed Brick on a ladder painting the side of the house. Brick raised one hand to acknowledge their presence, but kept on painting. John Tom saw Tom standing at the door and he immediately gave him a bear hug. Dottie graciously hugged Peggy 2. After the brief introduction, the foursome made their way into the parlor, but Brando and Dante stopped them at the parlor door. The dogs were standing in the doorway wagging their tails. Peggy 2 was the first to speak. She looked back at Tom without touching either dog.

"I didn't know you had dogs. I had dogs when I lived with mama and daddy, but we kept them outside. There were chocolate Lab's, I think. Kind of pretty things. What kind are these dogs?"

The dogs' voice came back. "She's like the dog that sets a whole street of dogs barking."

Tom got a funny feeling in his stomach as he studied her.

"English Bull dogs, Peggy. I'm sure bulldogs are in Tennessee, right?"

John Tom began pushing Peggy 2 into the parlor. He wanted to sit down. He knew Peggy 2 couldn't talk and walk at the same time without some kind of help. Peggy 2

Immediately went toward the sofa. Dottie and Tom didn't want to sit until they saw where the conversation might go, so they stood in front of the TV. John Tom answered his son as he took a seat in the recliner.

"Peggy doesn't know the difference between a cat and a dog. Peggy, Don and Jackie have a bulldog. You saw the bulldog last week, when we went to their house for dinner."

Peggy 2 looked confused. "Do what?"

John Tom repeated his thoughts in a louder voice.

"Oh, really? That dog looked different somehow. Are you sure? I know it wasn't no cat."

Peggy 2 gave John Tom a scowling look.

John Tom could feel his blood boiling. He knew Peggy 2 had memory issues unless she talked about her childhood years. She could remember everything that happened to her between the ages of 10 and 18, but what happened last week or last night was always a struggle. She fabricated stories. And the main characters in those stories were all people in her family. She had five children by two men, and they always came into a current conversation in some way. Her mama and daddy were main characters in her distorted stories as well.

John Tom had patience issues all his life. He blamed those is- sues on his early years as well as his naval service. He looked at his wife, and then raised his voice again to make his point.

"It's a bulldog Peggy. Don showed me his papers. His parents were cJohn Tompions show dogs."

Peggy 2 still looked confused. "Do what?"

John Tom's temper went into overload

mode.

"Get your ears checked when we get back will ya?"

Peggy 2 ignored John Tom's last statement.

"Oh, really? I thought it might be a boxer."

Tom realized the conversation kept moving nowhere. But before he could change the subject Dottie added more fuel to the fire.

"Brando and Dante come from a long line of cJohn Tompions. They are great dogs, but they can be a little messy."

Peggy 2 was on one of her rolls.

"My mama had two Beagles when she was young, and daddy had a big black Rottweiler in those days. He said that dog had a meanness, so his daddy kept him chained up all the time."

Dottie didn't like that image. Chaining a dog is like putting chains on a child in her mind.

"No wonder the dog had a mean streak. Dogs hate being chained all the time. Bet your mom didn't chain those Beagles, or did she?"

"She did too, but those two dogs were lazy and fat, so they didn't care much."

Dottie could feel the frustration percolating inside of her, so she changed the subject.

"Is this your first trip to California, Peggy?"

Before Peggy 2 could answer, Tom jumped in.

"Dad, do you want a beer?"

"Sure. Do you have Rolling Rock?"

Tom nodded.

"What would you like, Peggy?"

"Do y'all have sweet tea? It is my first trip to California. I've never been out of Tennessee."

Tom nodded again and left the room. From the look of things, the next two weeks could be a major lesson in patience for him.

The Rolling Rock started to shake in the green bottle as Tom handed it to his dad. He put the ice tea with three tablespoons of sugar in front of Peggy 2. John Tom took his first swig. and looked around the comfortable room. He noticed a picture of the girls.

"How are my beautiful girls doing?"

Tom looked at Dottie. Dottie was first to answer.

"Well, Tiffany is living in Oakland. She works for an advertising firm. Iris studies art at the University of the Arts in downtown Philly, and Erica is in her third year of high school."

Peggy 2 took a large sip of her tea and looked at Dottie.

"My granddaughter goes to college next year. That's some sweet tea. Y'all don't make it the way we do back home."

Tom kept his composure.

"We call it ice tea around here, Peggy. It's cold tea with sugar in it. How do you make it in Tennessee?"

Peggy took another sip, and she looked around the room before she answered the question. The room had Walt Disney memorabilia on the walls. Peggy 2 immediately focused on a picture of Walt Disney breaking ground for Disneyland. She immediately interrupted the conversation about the girls.

"Oh, I don't know. I guess the tea is the same. But it just tastes different."

She put her glass down and stared at one of the pictures.

"Is that Walt Disney up there in that picture? He looks young. My daddy kinda looked like him. He had a moustache too."

Tom's one nerve was about to explode as he heard the sound of her squeaky voice, but he still kept his composure.

"Yep, that's old Walt. That shot came from Dottie's uncle, Dick Kelsey. Dick worked as Walt's production artist in the forties and fifties. He played a big part in developing Magic Mountain theme park in Colorado as well."

Peggy 2 got up and walked around the room picking up different pictures.

"I bet all this work is worth a lot of money now. My mama had a picture of James Polk before he became president. I think that thing is worth something, if I could find it. John Tom made me put it somewhere, and I have no clue where."

John Tom couldn't resist. He had to stop her the only way he knew how.

"Peggy, you forget where your clothes are most of the time. God made idiots for practice, and then he made you, I guess."

Dottie thought John Tom's cold comments sucked, but she kept silent. Tom laughed out loud. His dad never minced words. If he felt annoyed, Tom let everybody know it.

Peggy 2 sat back down on the sofa and finished the last gulp of her tea. She looked at John Tom.

"The only reason I forget where some of my clothes are is I have so many. They are in that small closet, and I can't get to them. When I was living with mama I had a bigger closet, and I could find things much better."

Tom knew they had to get this new addition to his family out of the parlor.

"Why don't you two go up to your room and freshen up before we take a ride over to see Jake Ross? He wants to meet you, dad. Your room is the second door on the left when you reach the top of the stairs."

John Tom got up and Peggy 2 did too. John Tom's memory was not as good as it used to be, but it was better than Peggy 2's.

"Who is Jake Ross?

Tom looked at his father.

"I told you about him, dad. He's the guy I work out with. Jake's about your age."

His father shook his head in agreement.

"You look like you're in pretty good shape, Tom."

Peggy 2 chimed in.

"Oh, really? I'd like to meet him too. My daddy liked to walk on a treadmill before he passed. He had MS, but he still could walk a little."

John Tom heard enough from his girlfriend.

"Peggy, nobody cares about your daddy's treadmill. I swear you don't know the difference between the right words and the almost right words. You use the word lightning when you should be using lightning bug or the other way around."

"I'm not talking about bugs; I'm talking about exercise. That's what your son said anyway."

John Tom grabbed Peggy 2's arm.

"Forget it, Peggy. Let's go upstairs. I need a nap."

"You always need a nap when you're around me."

John Tom smiled as he walked up the creaky steps.

"I wish you were that smart all the time, Peggy."

Tom and Dottie grinned at each other and simultaneously started walking to the back porch.

"What the hell, Dot? Is she for real? She got to be slow in the brain. If her identity got ripped off, the thief would wind up a basket case. I don't know if I can keep my cool around her for the next two weeks."

159

Dottie laughed.

"Your dad seems annoyed with her. He said some mean things to her. I guess it's a test for both of us. I think the guests arriving tonight may be another test."

"What do you mean?"

"Well, it's four people from Utah. The man said he was a preacher, and he has three women with him. He only wanted one room."

"You got to be kidding? Are you going to put them in one room? I hope this doesn't turn into some kind of religious orgy. What about the old-fashion way before silly self-serving laws surfaced? You know the days when everyone thought e-coli was an after dinner drink."

Dottie didn't want to answer a lot of questions, but Tom continued.

"Do the women take turns in bed, or do they all sleep together? How long do they plan to stay?"

"I didn't ask them a lot of questions. But I did ask them when they wanted to check out. The preacher said it was for one night only. He told me they don't drink, and they only want a light breakfast in the morning. I think he said they live in Utah or Arizona. I put two and two together. I think they follow Mormon beliefs. I guess we have to respect their way of life. It's different, but we all are different. Thank God for that."

"Don't worry. I can't remember a single time when I was irreverent toward anything except the things that are reverent to other people."

"Thanks real funny. I think you are going to have your hands full with John Tom and that girlfriend of his. Do you think he will marry her?"

"Oh my God. Please tell me this is a dream. I'm not in the market for a step-mother — especially one like her."

The meeting with Jake went well. Dottie stayed at the B&B. Peggy 2 didn't say much, but she did say enough to show her ass. When she did open her mouth, she put her foot in it. But Jake was gracious enough to ignore most of her comments. After a brief exchange of gracious comments, Jake looked at John Tom and noticed he had a stocky build.

"If you lived out here, John Tom I would have you in top shape in six weeks. It looks like you have good muscle tone at your age. Your body structure is easy to work with."

John Tom looked at Jake and smiled.

"I'm in great shape for the shape I'm in, Jake. You know a man can't be comfortable with himself without his own approval, and I have plenty of self approval in me."

Peggy 2 looked at John Tom and then at Jake.

"The only exercise I get these days amounts to sleeping and eating. Mama use to say I could sleep better than anyone in Nashville, and I could eat any man under the table even when I was ten."

Jake looked at her and made a strange face. He wasn't sure if the woman with the 1950s teased hair style was serious or not. He looked at her outfit and realized her pink petal pusher pants and white sleeveless shirt resembled a 50s teenager's look. The only difference was her facial lines and wrinkles, hidden under what appeared to be an overdone make-up job.

"Now, you got to exercise especially as you get older, Peggy. I don't consider sleeping or eating exercise, but I'm not from the South. I guess you folks look at life a little different back there."

John Tom didn't want Peggy 2 to continue her senseless gibberish, so he cut her off.

"Peggy you never miss the opportunity to keep quiet until it ceases to be one. Jake doesn't want to hear about your strange habits or what your mama had to say."

Jake smiled, and nodded his head without saying a word.

Tom knew it was time to move on. He didn't want to endure anymore boring Peggy 2 stories especially around Jake.

"Jake we have to go, but I'll see you Monday."

Jake seemed relieved. He looked at John Tom and avoided Peggy 2.

"Nice to meet you folks." Come see me when you can stay a little longer, John Tom."

Jake never looked at Peggy 2 again.

When the trio got back to the B&B it was almost eight. John Tom felt sleepy, and Peggy 2 was still being her annoying self. Dottie had dinner waiting and the pair ate like there was no tomorrow. Tom wanted to make a comment, but he didn't. Dottie made sure he didn't by talking all through dinner. She talked about the girls and their accomplishments. Peggy 2 always added something boring about her kids after Dottie's comments.

John Tom finished his cup of black coffee, and Peggy 2 slurped a cappuccino. She put the tiny cup down and looked at Dottie.

"What time is breakfast in the morning, Dottie? Can I sleep a little bit? I think the time change got to me."

John Tom looked at her.

"It's not just the time change, Peggy. You brain wants to find a home that has some sense in it."

Tom laughed, and Dottie smiled.

"Come down when you get up, Peggy. I promise a gourmet breakfast when you come down. I have guests tonight. They plan to eat around 9, but if you get up before then that's okay too."

The exhausted couple finished their drinks, kissed and hugged their hosts and walked through the living room and up the stairs. As they walk through the living room, Peggy 2 accidently stepped on Brando's paw. The dog let out a shriek. Peggy 2 jumped forward, and landed sideways on one of the red wing-back chairs instead of the floor.

"My lord, I didn't see that thing laying there, John Tom. Why didn't you say something?"

"Come on, Peggy It's late our time. We'll get you some glasses when we get back home. But before we do, we will get you a brain transplant."

Peggy 2 slowly got up from the chair, and looked at Dottie and Tom. They tried to help her regain her balance.

Tom thought she just fell without any injuries, but Dottie thought she hurt her ankle.

"Are you alright, Peggy?"

"Mama told me to watch out for things. She said I always bumped into something and hurt myself. Guess she, well, you know. Mama and right were tight."

John Tom was halfway up the steps when he yelled.

"Come on Peggy. We have heard enough about your mama today."

Peggy quickly gained her composure and followed John Tom upstairs.

Tom looked at Dottie.

"I hope she doesn't come down for breakfast at the same time as the guests. That would be a recipe for disaster. I'm not sure I want to talk to that bunch this morning. What did you think when they arrived today?"

"All I can say, Tom is you may not want to be around to-morrow morning. Between the guests and your family, we may be in for a real goat rodeo. I can take it, but I know you might go off the deep end."

"Why because of Peggy 2?"

"No because of the guests. They have some interesting ideas about life and I don't think you will agree with them."

"Well you know me. I believe good breeding means concealing how much you think of your own beliefs and how little you think about the beliefs of others."

Dottie looked Tom and smiled.

"Okay, Okay but remember it's better to stay out of the conversation than to get in it. Once you're in the conversation, you never know where you will wind up. And from what I experienced with you that place may not be your first choice once you think about it."

165

Tom thought for a minute. Dottie hit the nail on the head. A preacher and three wives plus, his father and his psychological basket case girlfriend may not make good breakfast company.

"You know you have a point. I'll work late tonight, so I can sleep in and miss all that insanity."

"Good thinking. Spending the day with your future step-mother put some sense in your head."

Tom shook his head as he walked toward the back porch.

"Dottie, the recipe for insanity is a little ignorance mixed in with a healthy dose of stupidity. I'm afraid old Peggy 2 has too much of both. She passed insanity while she headed to the funny farm for freaks. As dad said, the only sense she has is senselessness."

"That's not nice, dear. She does act like your dad's girlfriend."

"I know. And it worries me. An enemy can partly ruin a man, but it takes a senseless, injudicious companion to complete the task."

"Ha Ha! Go to work, Tom. Talk to you in the morning."

"Good night, Dottie. Thanks for being such a sense-filled companion."

"Thanks for noticing, Tom.

Chapter 13

You can't mold everybody the way you want them to be in life. Sometimes folks are just plain ignorant and they like themselves that way.

Unknown

Dottie always got up around five in the morning to prepare her gourmet breakfast. She wanted to sleep in some mornings, but she never did. She had a strange feeling this morning. But she didn't let those thoughts interrupt her, while she prepared semolina pancakes with honey, apricot jam instead of syrup, and her banana-bran muffins. She put the finishing touch on a batch of her strawberry and kiwi breakfast smoothies, and she had a pot of her famous hazelnut coffee brewing.

The first guest to walk through the living room was the preacher. The old mantle clock confirmed nine o'clock.

Dottie put two glasses filled with the morning smoothie on the table.

"Good morning, John. May I call you John?"

John J. Brown Jr. walked up to the head of the table, and pulled out the multicolored fabric covered chair. John was no lightweight. But his receding hairline, pot belly, and gray hair made him look older than his forty-one-years. Dottie thought that living with three wives was the catalyst for his appearance, but she didn't express those thoughts.

"Yes, of course, Dot. I don't like formal titles. I sure did get a good night sleep in that queen bed. And the room didn't make a sound. I know my wives sleep well, too."

Dottie thought for a few seconds before she answered. She couldn't understand how four people could sleep comfortably in that queen size bed. She also thought he didn't care if everyone knew he was a polygamist.

"Oh good. I thought you might be a little crowded. Do you have some sort of sleeping system that works for all of you? Then she remembered the big sleeping pillow in the closet.

Brown didn't like to talk about bedroom behavior, so he changed the subject.

"Do you have any other guests this morning, Dot?"

"Yes. My father-in-law and his friend are staying with us for two weeks. They may be down for breakfast soon."

Before Brown could ask another question the three women joined him around the table. Dottie acknowledged them as they entered the room.

"Good morning ladies. Who wants coffee and a smoothie? I think I remember everyone's name from last night."

"Good morning." The reply was in choir harmony.

Libby was the first to speak.

"We all drink coffee, and we would love a smoothie.

Thank you, Dottie."

Dottie looked at each woman. The tall one with jet black hair and the extended midriff looked to be about thirty-five. John called her Jessie. Maxine was the short, thin one with long blonde hair and an angelic-looking face. Dottie thought she was about thirty. Libby the stocky, black woman was the spokesman for the group. She didn't smile as she took seat on the right side of John. None of the woman wore makeup and all of them were dressed in white cotton dresses that covered their knees. Libby's dress seemed longer than the others. Dottie couldn't tell how old she was, but she thought she was well over forty.

Dottie disappeared into the kitchen, and as she did Tom came out of their bedroom and made his presence known.

"Good morning folks. It looks like a beautiful day. Were you all comfortable last night?"

Brown looked at the girls and then at Tom.

"Indeed, Mr. Donovan. We love your home. Our house is not as big as this one, but it is Victorian style."

"Dottie said you lived in Utah. Do you live around Salt Lake?"

"We live in Colorado City, Arizona. It sits right across the Utah state line. We belong to the Fundamental

Latter Day Saint Church, and we are out here on a mission trip. We want to spread the word of Christ in some of the Indian settlements around here. You know those folks need to know about heaven and hell and Jesus, right?"

Tom didn't like to get into this kind of conversation with guest because he knew it wouldn't end well. Dottie heard part of the conversation while she was getting the coffee. She knew things might get out of hand especially before Tom had his special pomegranate-blueberry smoothie. Tom looked at the women and then at Brown.

"Well, I don't like to give my opinion on heaven and hell because I think I have friends in both places."

The women laughed, but Brown didn't.

"Let me explain Brother Donovan. We believe in the word of God, which came from a divine revelation given to Brother John Taylor in 1886. Brother Lorin C. Woolley wrote a paper about that revelation in 1912. Many doctrines came out of that 1886 manifesto."

Tom knew he was in for another ride on the wacko roller coaster. He couldn't let this challenge go. He had to respond even though Dottie gave him the evil eye as she put coffee and a smoothie in front of the women.

"Well I know one thing for sure John, and you just confirmed it. In religion and in politics too, people's beliefs and truths are almost always received second hand. And for the most part never questioned."

Brown didn't like what Tom said. But he heard his stomach make some hungry noises, so he kept quiet for a second. Then he thought Tom was just another California heretic that needed saving.

"I tell you, brother. We have many great prophets. They all speak to the Lord and spread his word. The Word is true and unfiltered. The Book of Mormon is the scripture and we live by it. And we want the rest of the world to live by it too."

"No offense John, but I think people get confused by some of the passages in any Scripture, especially when they don't understand them. But what bothers me are the passages I do understand."

Dottie grabbed Tom by the arm and asked him to help her in the kitchen. She had to get him out of the dining room. She saw Peggy 2 and John Tom walking through the living room and into the dining room. Dottie pulled him to the door near the back porch.

"I thought you were going to sleep late this morning. You know better than to discuss religion with the guests. Quit,

Tom. I mean it."

Tom didn't want to upset his wife.

"Okay, I saw dad come in so I'll talk to him. I hope Peggy 2 can keep her mouth shut this morning. If she starts preaching, I might look like a saint in front of this group."

"Never mind all that, Tom. Here take a smoothie and a muffin to your dad and Peggy 2."

Dottie picked up the two cups of coffee and followed Tom into the dining room. Peggy 2 and John Tom sat at the far side of the table. John Tom started to ask John a question as she put the smoking hot coffee in front of him.

"It's funny that you're here. Peggy and I watched a movie the other night about a wagon train massacre. We love westerns."

Peggy 2 interrupted her husband.

"I always watched John Wayne movies, but I don't think he was in this one right, John Tom?"

John Tom looked around the table and saw confused faces.

"Peggy, we not talking about John Wayne right now, and no he wasn't in this movie."

Peggy 2 didn't listen to John Tom's answer. "Daddy always liked John Wayne." John Tom raised his voice.

"Never mind her, folks. She remembers everything whether it happened or not. I guess you all know how dumb the average person can be. Multiply that by two, and you got a good handle on Peggy's brain."

Brown and the women laughed as John Tom continued.

"What I would like to know, and I hope you understand my question. What really happened at Mountain Meadows in Utah back in 1857? Hard to believe Mormons would kill folks passing through on a wagon train. The movie showed your people dressing up like Indians and killing every one of those people in cold blood. I think a few children survived, but the rest of them, over 120 people, met their maker that day."

The room went silent. Tom put the smoothie in front of John Tom and Peggy 2 and walked over to the buffet. John looked at John Tom, and then at Peggy 2. He took a sip of coffee, and made a face. And then wiped his mouth with the cloth napkin.

"I'm surprised you know about that, sir. It was a dark time for the Mormon faith. The Utah War raged on at that time, and our militia had war fever. They thought invaders want to take their land, and they wanted to stop these intruders. The militia that participated in that incident did have memberships in the Latter Day Saints congregation — not the Fundamentalists movement we follow."

John Tom didn't give up.

"I did a little research after the movie. I don't think there was a difference back then, right? I think Brother Tom Young was a little paranoid, don't you think?"

John quickly responded.

"Brother Young did not face any charges. A jury found Mr. John D. Lee guilty, and he was put to death. It was a dark time in our history. I can assure you we are peaceful folks. We follow the Word to the letter."

The dogs' voice was back. "People act in strange ways, but as you can see strange doesn't seem wrong to them."

Tom tried to bring some of his rational thoughts into the conversation.

"We all like to hear about the dark side in others. Stories like that make us feel normal. Violence and war seems like normal behavior. The forces of evil seem to find their way into everyone's house. Religion kind of brings it on, in my opinion."

Dottie saw the nervousness in her guests. She signaled Tom, and they returned to the kitchen to get the pancakes and banana-bran muffins. She looked at Tom.

"You know Tom no word is better than a perfectly timed pause. You might want to practice your pausing skill a little more. That conversation is going nowhere fast."

As soon as she said that she heard the women laughing. She heard John laugh above the rest. She grabbed four plates of pancakes and put two on each arm. She couldn't wait to hear what was so funny.

Tom brought a basket filled with the muffins and put it in the middle of the table. He looked at his father.

"These are the best muffins in Northern California, Dad. I heard all the laughter. Did Peggy share some of her humor with the group?"

"You might say that, son. She asked Jessie how she stayed so thin. Jessie said she eats what she wants, and then she lets the food fight it out on the inside."

Peggy 2 looked at Jessie, and then she looked at Libby.

"Libby, do you help with the chores? My mama had a black woman friend, and she helped her keep the house clean and all."

Once again the table went silent. Libby stared at Peggy and got the feeling she wasn't right in the head.

"Well Peggy, you could say I work for the family. I'm John's first wife."

Libby smiled, and the rest of the group shook their heads in agreement. After that exchange, the group finished eating and didn't say a word. John Tom and Peggy 2 did the same. The conversation was way over in Brother John's mind. He knew he couldn't save anyone in that house. They marched to another drummer, and he didn't like the music.

When the group finished, they quietly put their napkins on the plate in front of them, and waited for John to get up.

175

When he did, the women followed him. John looked at John Tom and Peggy 2.

"Nice meeting you. May the Lord bless you brother and sister."

John Tom shook John's hand. And he nodded to each woman as they passed by him. Peggy 2 stood there with a silly grin on her face.

Tom and Dottie thanked the group, and Tom followed them out the door. Tom wanted to get the last word in. He didn't understand their mission, but he knew better than question it especially in front of Dottie.

"Hope you enjoy the rest of your trip. Give my regards to the folks in Sherwood Valley. I think you'll learn a lot from them. They know the real meaning of the Word. They live it every day."

John turned around and looked down at Tom.

"I want to teach them the real Word, brother Donovan. I call them poor heathens. They are lost in their own devilish world."

Tom decided not to push it. He smiled and thanked them once again and went inside.

The dogs spoke again "A lie can travel halfway around the world while the truth is still putting on its shoes."

Chapter 14

I never learned hate at home. I had to go to school for that.

Dick Gregory

The dogs'voice seemed louder than before. "Some days you're the dog and some days you're the fire hydrant."

2008 was another crucial year for the Donovan family. Tom's business started to slowdown, and the Bed and Breakfast didn't have the normal backlog of guests. The financial crash hit them hard. And the Donovan's, like millions of other families, didn't have the cash reserves to weather the crisis without losing something. The mortgage on the B&B was a challenge, and the other expenses put them in financial jeopardy. Tom teetered on the edge of disaster, and he knew it. One morning after his usual breakfast of muffins and pomegranate-blueberry juice, he got up from his desk, and walked into the kitchen. Dottie was on the phone talking to her neighbor, Millie.

"Oh, I don't know, Millie. We're not going to try to sell this place. No one is buying anything. The banks turned their backs on working people. Tom and I will figure something out. We always do."

Tom stood in the kitchen and watched their massive turtle eat a pile of grass and dead flowers in the backyard. One ear tuned-in into his wife's conversation, and the other one did not hear anything. He watched the family pet Munch, and then move away from his breakfast feast. Suddenly a thought jumped through his mind.

"Dottie we got to talk, now."

Dottie held up her hand signaling him to stop talking.

"Sorry Millie. Say that again. Tom was trying to butt-in."

Dottie listened to her friend for a minute.

"No, no we'll be alright. But I might need you later this week. Love you."

Dottie hung up the phone. She seemed annoyed by Tom's lack of patience.

"What is it, Tom? Is it so important it couldn't wait until I finished talking to Millie?"

"Sorry Honey, but the turtle just gave me an idea."

"Please, tell me you're not serious, Tom. I know that turtle can do a lot of things, but talking is not one of them."

Tom smiled.

He thought of the word courage. He remembered what someone said to him in school—*Courage is the mastery of fear; the resistance of fear, not the absence of fear. He forgot that until just now. The solution is on the other side of every problem. You just have to focus on the solution."*

Dottie thought for a minute.

"I thought the only thing you said you learned in school was how to hate and how to be devious."

"That's funny, but you know me. I'm not one to express my opinions using just facts. I'm creative you know."

Dottie smiled and saw a spark in her husband's eye. He was ready to fight to keep what they worked for all these years.

"Okay so what's your plan?

"I'm going to get a job."

"In this economy? Are you shitting me, Tom?"

The phone rang before Tom could answer Dottie. He picked up the receiver.

"Hello, President's Bed and Breakfast this is Tom."

"Hi Tom. It's Frank Rainwater."

Tom hadn't talked to Frank in over two years.

"Hey Frank. How's the family?"

"We are all good and thankful, Tom. I'm calling to let you know that a friend of mine in Pleasantville needs a new computer programmer. He is a member of my tribe. He started a business a couple of years ago. Mr. Dakota writes programs for grocery stores. He got a grant from the government, so his business is well capitalized. And it's growing steadily even in this economy. I thought you might be interested in talking with him."

"Wow, Frank. I can't believe you called right now. I just told Dottie that I need another job. Do you think I would have to move to Pleasantville?"

"I asked Awan about that, and he said the programmer could work from his own office or home. That's why I called you. It sounds like something you could do right away. His name is Awan Dakota. His phone number is 510-555-4586. Remind him that we use to work together. I already told him you would call."

"Thanks, Frank. I'll call him right away. I do need work. Dottie and I were just discussing our present debacle. It would be great if you and Koi could come for dinner one Friday night? We would love to catch up and have a few laughs."

"Koi and I would like that. I'll call you in a couple of weeks. Koi and I are helping a family member deal with some personal stuff right now."

"Oh, I understand. Thanks again, Frank. I'll call you in a few weeks."

Dottie heard the conversation, and she could not believe it.

"Did Frank just give you the name of a guy that needs a computer guru?"

"You bet he did. See, I told you the turtle looks out for us. The turtle is a sacred animal in the Pomo culture. He probably got hold of Frank telepathically, or something?"

"Really, Tom? I never thought you would think like that. You believe that a turtle can communicate with a human? When did that metamorphosis that place?"

"I don't know. I guess my radical side shows when I'm stressed. You know radicals become conservatives over time. Radicals create the social storm, and when the winds of that storm die down, the conservatives adopt their ideas."

"I can't believe you keep saying that about yourself."

"I know, but it's true. But, I still don't understand why I never see headlines that read: *Psychic wins the lottery*."

"You know why, Mister. You still think you can win the

lottery." Tom laughed.

"Very funny, Dottie."

Right after the phone call from Frank, the judge called to book a room for three weeks. Ten minutes later Brie Miller called and booked a week-long stay.

Dottie hung up the phone and looked at Tom.

"What's up? It seems like all our friends are in rescue mode. I guess it's all that good karma we built up over the years."

Tom nodded.

"I don't know about karma, but there is something strange about these back-to-back calls. I'm holding my breath right now. I hope the next call is not from Hazel or Ruth."

Dottie felt a twinge run down her spine.

"Let's not talk about them right now. I'm sure they have their own problems. I bet Todd's business got hit by the meltdown. I know they will be okay, but Hazel might think the end of the world is on the way. I don't want to hear her rant-on about how bad life is when she is in better shape financially than most of us. And you know Ruth; she'll find comfort in the arms of another or in the laps of many."

Tom agreed.

"Hazel doesn't know how to empathize when others struggle with challenges. She makes her situation worse, so she is the center of attention. She reminds me of Peggy 2. Ruth just looks for love in all the wrong places. She has to find it within her first."

"Wow, Tom. Are you reading those self-help books again? The last time I heard you talk like that was when Brie stayed here the last time. Ok, let's change the subject. I don't want to talk about my family or yours."

Tom got quiet. His dad popped into his mind. He still had a hard time believing his dad married Peggy 2 in Vegas on their way back to Nashville after their visit in 2003. How could he be so stupid? When the postcard came in the mail, he almost threw up. There was a picture of his dad and Peggy 2 on a mechanical bull. The note under the photo said: *It's no bull, we got married!*

"Tom, wake-up. You're in dreamland"

Tom snapped out of it.

"Sorry, the word family put me orbit."

"Well, get back to Earth. We got things to do before you make that call to Pleasantville."

The call to Awan Dakota went better than expected. Tom got the job. But a one-on-one meeting in Pleasantville the following Monday would close the deal. Frank told Awan Tom could start right away. Awan needed a person right away. Awan landed the Kroger Food account, and he needed an experienced programmer.

"It looks like he wants to hire me subject to a personal interview, Dot. Do you think I should wear my suit for the meeting?"

"No. That's suit has moth holes in it. Why not go Mervyns and buy a new one?"

"Okay. I have $100 tucked away for a rainy day. I'll use it on a new suit."

"Good thinking. What would the world do without you, Tom? Better yet what would you do without you?"

Tom smiled and started swinging his arms and moving his torso. He had an unusual rhythm going on in his body. Dottie cracked up.

"What the hell, Tom? Have you been bitten by a spider or something?"

"No. I'm happy so I'm doing the elevator dance."

"Elevator dance? What's that?"

"It's a dance with no steps."

She turned and walk out of the room.

"Really, Tom? Really?

Chapter 15

Does one thing lead to another? Not always. Sometimes one thing leads to the same thing. Ask an addict.

George Carlin

About a year went by before the Donovan's had dinner with the Rainwater's. Koi and Frank stayed active in their community as well as with their family. They didn't get a chance to socialize with people outside of that network. But, they made an exception. They wanted to see Dottie and Tom, and they wanted to share experiences in their colorful world. Dottie decided to invite Walt and Millie and Brink and Dana.

Dottie hugged Koi as she walked through the front door. Frank and Tom did a man hug and smiled as they exchanged "*hey man how you doing.*" The couples immediately went into the living and sat down. As soon as they sat down, the other two couples walked through the front door. Frank and Tom got up, but Koi and Dottie kept their seats. The couples exchanged greetings and Tom got them all something to drink.

As he did he heard Koi's voice.

"It's great to see you, Dottie. Where are those pretty dogs of yours?"

Tom heard the voice again. "No one appreciates the special genius in human's conversation like we do."

Koi and Dottie had a strong connection to all animals. Dottie spent hours healing wounded wild animals, and Koi helped her on a few occasions over the years.

"Brando and Dante sleep in the bedroom. That's what they do most of the time. Old age slows them down, and they both have arthritis."

Koi's face showed her concern.

"Oh so sorry, Dottie. I know you will take care of them the best way."

Tom, Frank and the others listened to the conversation. Frank loved those dogs.

"We've had a lot of death around us the last couple of years. My buddy Jake died of a heart attack last year, and two of our regular guests died last month. My best friend from Philly died of cancer two months ago. And one of Dottie's helper had a stroke, and died last week, so we are up to our necks in death at the moment."

Frank spoke up.

"Don't forget Max. His cold heart finally stopped eight months ago."

Koi shook her head in agreement. The others sat quietly as Tom continued sharing his thoughts.

"Oh, right, Frank. I don't mean to be so morbid, but I have a hard time dealing with people dying. Ever since my mother died, the death of anyone near me turns into an upsetting, and unnerving experience. I don't know if my age has something to do with it, or I'm just paranoid."

Koi looked at Frank, and then she turned to Tom.

"It's not death that makes you paranoid, Tom. It is your belief about it. My people believe that death is a new beginning. We believe the spirit goes through a period of peace. Then the soul experiences what it believed it would experience in death, when the soul was in the body. That's why we call death a new life. We make it what we want. We can choose to reincarnate again, or we can stay in the peace. In my world, death is the doorway that leads to the region of choices."

Tom made a funny face.

"I never thought about death that way. My religion and my mother's religion taught me to believe in heaven, hell, and atonement for my sins."
Koi continued expressing her beliefs.

"Those thoughts overflow with fear. No God would separate, judge, and convict itself. God is us. He's not sitting somewhere picking sides or keeping score. We are one, but we have choices and beliefs, when we are in a body. The white man's beliefs restrict and put limits on his spirit. But, the spirit has no limits. Just like in the dream
187

world. That is the Pomo way. All life is an experience in spirit. That spirit knows no sin. Fear creates sin."

Dottie shook her head up and down and looked at Tom. Walt smiled and said: "Amen." Brink and Dena looked perplexed, but Dena wanted to comment.

"You know Koi I never thought about life that way, but I think I know what you mean. I sense it while I'm dancing, and when I'm with my pets. Plus, I see it my garden every day."

Frank smiled, and so did Brick. He looked at Tom and then, Koi. Frank wanted to add his thoughts too.

"Many white men tried to take our beliefs away from us. They all still have the mentality that if the Calvary won it was a great victory. But if the Indians won, it was a massacre. We act like savages according to some of your people. We still have people coming to our land with bibles and crosses. These religious people want us to be as fearful as they are. Our ancestors taught us to believe in our choices and respect the choices of others. That is the way of the spirit."

Tom thought for a minute.

"I think I know what you mean. We had a group from Arizona stay here a year or two ago, and they told us they wanted to save you from your beliefs."

Koi nodded her head.

188

"Many come, Tom, but they always leave with more to think about. The group you speak about didn't stay long at the ranch. My people showed them what heaven on earth looks like. My people treated them with respect, but they did not think we were smart enough to know the ways of heaven. The big man with three wives said we were doomed to hell. We don't believe in heaven or hell."

Dottie got up and excused herself. She knew Koi and Frank beliefs made sense.

Dottie's version of a vegan Asian salad was a hit, and her chicken divine satisfied Tom's meat cravings. Frank, Walt, and Brick had a little of both, so the meal and the tiramisu desert hit the spot. Dottie offered everyone her signature hazelnut coffee with desert, but the women wanted tea.

After another hour of laughs and interesting conversation The Sensinger's and the Morgan's excused themselves and left the Rainwater's sitting in the living room with the Donovan's.

Koi wanted to share a personal experience that touched her family in a very unusual way, but she wanted to wait until the other couples went home. It was very personal to her, but she knew Dottie was a friend without judgment. Koi took a sip of tea, and then crossed her legs in front of her. Frank knew what happens next, but he didn't say a word. Tom admired Koi's native dress and moccasins as she started to express herself.

189

"My older sister, Abey has a twenty-eight -year-old son named Hute. He married a white girl from Sacramento, and they moved into a house near my sister. The couple had a baby boy at the end of last year. They refused to let anyone hold him. Even my mother could not hold or even get near the baby.

Dottie had a shocked look on her face.

"What's wrong with that girl? Did her parents ever hold the baby?"

Koi shook her head.

"No, she will not allow her parents to come unless they call first. Her parents visited once since the birth. Visitors must wear a mask and gloves in the baby's room. Do you know of any child that would not allow a grandparent the gift of being a grandparent?"

Tom looked out the window and saw an almost full moon. Dottie took a sip of her tea.

"I didn't think anyone could be that callous did you, Tom?"

"It makes me want to create a hotline for people who don't want advice in the first place."

Dottie couldn't hold her tongue.

"It sounds like she needs help. And it looks like someone needs to have a come-to-Jesus meeting with Hute."

Koi looked puzzled.

"Come-to-Jesus meeting, Dottie? Do you mean a serious talk of some kind? We call this talk a meeting of spirits. My sister and her husband do not want to push them farther away, so they are silent. I think I should talk to them. What do you think?"

Dottie looked at Tom. Tom didn't hesitate. He wanted to break the tension.

"Let me talk to them, Koi. I'll give them some excellent advice. I'm trained in enduring adversity—another man's adversity."

Dottie quickly shot fire from her eyes, and it landed on Tom.

'Never mind all that, Tom. This is serious. The only thing we can do is help find a solution by doing a little research. Let's talk to Louie Saltscrewber when he gets here tomorrow. He's a psychologist, and he specializes in family issues."

"Good idea, Dot."

Tom wanted the conversation to end, and so did Dottie. In one way, Koi didn't like talking about this topic, but in another way she felt relieved.

"Please forgive me. I guess it shows you we all are human with different feelings. The teaching of our ancestors sits under the ignorance of the modern world. It's sad to think that way."

Frank and Koi got up and hugged their hosts. They had nothing more to say. The two couples knew they had a strong bond, and it had nothing to do with race. They were brother and sisters in this new world.

The next afternoon was a busy one. Tom had extra programming work, and he also had to help Brick paint the second floor of the house. Dottie's mission was to talk to Dr. Saltscrewber. Saltscrewber arrived around four that afternoon. He wore his signature multi-colored blue striped bow tie, blue linen suit, and his well-worn off-white ascot cap. His gray hair exposed in a short ponytail. His blue eyes hid under a pair of Foster Grant sunglasses. His suit coat remained open because his belly's spare tire inflated over two inches in the last two years. He blamed his diet for the weight gain, but lack of physical exercise certainly played a role in his Raymond Burr type physique. When he saw Dottie standing at the door, he quickly dropped his 1940s brown calf leather Pullman bag on the floor and gave her a hug.

"Hey Dottie. How y'all doing. I tried to remember the last time I was here, but I think my memory is a little weak at the moment."

Dottie loved Louie. His gracious Southern accent, and his formal, but ruffled attire made her smile every time she saw him. Saltscrewber usually came once a year to talk at the college, but three years passed since his last stay.

"Oh, it's well over three years, Louie. We sure missed your company. Hope all is well with you and the family."

"Just fine, Dottie. Just fine. Where's old Tom? I've got a couple of stories for him."

Dottie pick up his suitcase and began talking while she walked upstairs.

"Tom's doing a little manual labor. Let me show you to your room. You're in the Roosevelt Room this time. I know you love to sit by the window and write, don't you?"

"I do, indeed. I appreciate your hospitality."

"It's a pleasure, Louie. After you freshen up, please come down and have some tea in the living room. I want to ask you a professional question."

"That's a deal, Dot. I'll be down in thirty minutes. I want to wash some of this California olive juice off my skin. You know what I mean?"

Dottie laughed.

"I do know. Tom's been trying to get it off his skin for the last fifteen years."

They both laughed. Saltscrewber felt at home at the B&B. It always seemed like a homecoming. He took off his jacket. And kicked off his black and white two-tone wing tips and pulled out his computer. He sat down at the table by the bay window and began typing. He typed the words: *Family Issues* at the top of the page and stopped. Saltscrewber's eyes closed and five minutes later the sound of his own snoring woke him up. He pushed himself up from the chair and went to the antique-inspired bathroom. He turned the hot water on, and gave himself a wash basin bath. Immediately he felt refreshed. A cup of tea would seal his freshness, he thought.

Louie entered the living room dressed the same way. He did leave his cap, jacket, sunglasses and bag in his room. But the bow tie, his suit pants and his wingtips were his signature look.

Dottie had a cup of jasmine tea waiting for him, and a plate packed with chocolate filled cookies.

"I thought you might like a sugar boost before dinner, Louie. I made these this morning."

"Well thank you. I do need a pick-me-up right about now. I don't like to eat before nine your time. That's seven my time."

Louie sat in black antique rocking chair and took a sip of his tea.

Tom walked in and shook Louie's hand.

"How the hell are you, Louie. How's everything in Mississippi?"

"About the same, Tom. The state is still last in the race to educate. But you know, anyone can become president in this country."

Tom laughed and watched Louie picked up his tea and look at Dottie.

"What's on your mind, Dot?"

Dottie started the story the same way Koi did the night before. She felt her eyes filling up with tears during her monologue, but she held them back. Saltscrewber listened intently to Dottie's version of the mom and dad that wouldn't let anyone hold their baby. When she finished, he put down his cup, and wiped his mouth and hands with his napkin.

"Well, this kind of behavior happens all the time. We know race has nothing to do with it, and we know age is not a factor either. Parents of any age can choose to behave in any manner they like, when it comes to their newborn. Researchers really don't know the cause.
Some say post-partum depression may be a factor; others say parental fear plays a role. Some parents think the world is a big germ haven and everyone is a germ carrier. Even grandparents could carry harmful germs in the minds of these folks."

Dottie thought Louie's comments made sense. Any one of those things could create the situation Koi described.

Tom turned to Louie.

"I guess most people with that kind of low-self-esteem have earned it, right Louie?"

Louie laughed and Dottie immediately spoke up.

"What do you think, Louie? Have you studied and treated this kind of family behavior?"

Louie took a big bite of a chocolate cookie and a sip of tea. He shook his head as he tried to swallow his snack.

"I had one or two cases like that. I think it's a combination of things that create this kind of disorder, and it is a disorder. This disorder revolves around fear. Fear of being a new parent, fear of germs, fear of someone hurting the baby unintentionally. And fear they don't want the baby to go through the same kind of family experience they did. The other factor involves control. They want to control the baby early on, so the baby has a routine, and will conform to the rules of their correct behavior. They put themselves in the baby's situation. And they think their lives would be different if they had the same sort of structure they offer the baby."

Louie took another sip of tea. Dottie looked out the side window. Tom looked at Dottie and then at his guest.

Louie's thoughts started to sink in. Fear and control are dangerous bedfellows. Tom knew them intimately.

The dogs 'voice was active again. "The average dog is nicer than the average human. "

"Fear and control certainly make life tough, right Louie?"

"They do. That's what I'm going to talk about at the college tomorrow."

 "That's heavy stuff, Louie. Every family develops their own values and beliefs, right?"

Saltscrewber smiled.

"Yes, indeed. They want to enjoy their experiences through their child, and they will."

Tom smiled.

"I know parenthood is the only state where you can experience heaven and hell at the same time."

Louie laughed.

"Precisely! Raising kids is part fun and part warfare."

Dottie laughed as she got up from the sofa.

"You're right about that, Louie. I'm going to call my friend right now, and let her know what I know now. Thanks for sharing your wisdom, Louie. I know she will appreciate your input."

"My pleasure, Dottie."

Dottie raced toward the kitchen. Just like those young parents, she believed she could help Koi by sharing this new information. Louie got up and raised his voice.

"Thanks for the tea and cookies, Dottie. See you in the morning."

Thank you, Louie. You're the best!"

Chapter 16

How dare you look like someone I hate?

The Three Stooges

In 2011, Tom could believe his almost 57-year-old self. His thinning brown hair turned completely grey, and his long beard followed suit. The girls wanted him to shave the beard, but his beard fit his personality now, and so did his 248 lb. body. He stopped pumping iron when Jake died, so some of his muscle turned to fat. He struggled to walk because his heart was out of rhythm, and his blood pressure was at an all-time high. Tom had two partially blocked arteries, but he didn't know it. Dottie wanted him to make an appointment to see Dr. Rhonda Epperson, but he kept putting her off.

"Doesn't it bother you that Rhonda calls her work a practice? Hey, no one practices on me, Dot."

He wanted to handle his health issues with CO enzyme Q10 and a few other store bought remedies.

When Iris pulled up in front of the B&B that Saturday morning in July, Dottie and Tom didn't expect her. Their second child worked as an artist in a suburb of Oakland. She also volunteered at an animal shelter in Berkeley, so she usually only visited every three months. When Iris got out of her car, Tom and Walt stood by the side entrance of the B&B. They

Talk about the results of the 2010 election. Walt was a Jerry Brown supporter, and Tom was a Republican albeit a disgruntle one. He thought that Arnold would make a bigger impact on some of what he called the "stupid laws" in California while in office. But Schwarzenegger lived up to the saying "all Governors are geniuses when the economy rocks, and dunces when it goes sour." Arnold had a 23% approval rating when he left office. In Tom's mind that rating should be much lower. Tom was about to let Walt know that Brown was worse than Arnold thanks to his recent law changes. Those changes made him want to throw up, but Iris distracted him.

"Hi Honey, What in the world? Is that a new puppy?"

Iris was carrying a six-week old Pit Bull/Great Dane mix in her arms.

"Hi Daddy! Hi Mr. Sensinger! Surprise! I found this beautiful boy at the shelter. I knew you and mom would want him. I know you really miss Brando and Dante."

The dogs' voice got a little louder. We loved you and the family more than you loved yourself.

The bulldogs passed away within three weeks of each other back in January. The Donovan's took their deaths hard. Tom kissed his daughter, and she gently put the puppy in his arms.

"Hey big guy. You're a pretty boy aren't you?"

Dottie came out the side door when she heard the voices outside.

"Hey Honey! Oh my god, a new baby."

Dottie took the puppy out of Tom's arms.

"Come here sweetie. Look at those eyes and his markings, Tom. A grey and white pit with those markings is a great look. Wait a minute. He looks like Petey in the old Our Gang movies, right?"

Tom shook his head in agreement. "Let

me think of a name. Maybe something

rugged, Dot?"

"Oh yeah, he looks like a rock. Let's call him Stallone."

Tom looked at Iris and smiled.

"Yeah, I'll bet he'll answer to Stallone. He does look a little like Stallone."

Walt laughed and so did Iris. The Donovan's had a dog again. The B&B wasn't the same without dogs around. Stallone immediately became part of the family. Dottie and Iris went inside with the pup, and Walt and Tom continued their conversation.

"I'll be right in, Dottie. I want to finish what I started with old Walt while my blood pressure is still in the high position."

"The only thing old I see out there is you, dear."

Tom laughed, and said

"Well you're right. This is the oldest version of me to date, Dot."

Tom looked at Walt again.

"Okay. Tell me why you think Brown will be any better than Arnold iron body? He changed the law, so cops can't impound unlicensed driver's vehicles at DUI checkpoints. You know most of those habanero lovers might be illegal immigrants don't you?"

Walt got a serious look on his face.

"Well, they still can't drive the car. They have to call a friend or relative to drive the car away. They have rights too, Tom. Human rights checkmate our politically motivated laws, and Brown relates to that kind of thinking."

"I'm tired of people not taking responsibility for their actions. Driving without a license is not self-responsible behavior. I'm sick of people blaming the government for trying to force a little self-responsibility down their throats. That law does make sense, and so does our right to carry guns in public. When he outlawed handguns in public places, I couldn't hold back; I had to write a letter. We all have a right to bear arms, my friend. I bet Jerry has a gun hidden behind his statue of Buddha at the mansion."

"Tom, California is not the wild west anymore. I don't want urban cowboys coming in a restaurant or movie with a gun in a holster. That kind of life belongs in the 19th century."

Tom had a blank look on his face.

"Did you say you would choose to live in the 19th century, Walt? If you can make that kind of choice, I should have the right to choose to carry a gun wherever I want."

"It's not the same, Tom." There's more people now, and what about the kids? I know you don't want your girls going places where guns are a fashion statement. I think people have the right to own guns, but I don't think they should carry one to the grocery store. You know I talk about this on my radio show all the time, don't you?"

"Sorry Walt. I don't listen to your show. But, I did listen once."

Walt smiled.

"What was I talking about?"

"You talked about the Dream Act Part 2. You said you agreed with allowing illegal immigrants to receive tax-payer funded aid for college tuitions. And then when another guy asked if you gave a thumbs up for allowing cellphone searches without a warrant for anyone arrested.

you said— you know I am."

After that comment, I knew my blood pressure would not be able to handle your show on a daily basis. No offense, Walt you're a good neighbor, but a lousy conservative."

"Thank you, Tom. I scored a goal, if you think that way. I always like to give my opinion to wise voters."

"A word to the wise ain't the thing to do, Walt. It's the stupid ones who need advice. I think your comments feed a bunch of unwise-stupid folks a meal full of socialism."

"You know what Schumpeter said don't you, Tom?"

"What and who is Schumpeter?"

"Joe Schumpeter was a 20th century political scientist and economist. He served as finance minister of Austria in the early 1900s. Old Joe said that all capitalistic governments must eventually adapt some form of socialism. We are seeing the beginning phase of that process here in California."

"There is something fascinating about liberals, Walt. I really get a wholesome return of conjecture out of such a small investment of facts."

Walt had a sarcastic look on his face.

"I've got to go, Tom. It's been a pleasure. Let's do this again real soon."

"Don't worry, we will. You do give me something to think about."

"What's that, Tom?"

"If I ever think like one of your majorities, I'll know it's time for me to reform my opinions. If I don't get a compliment from you concerning my opinions I'm not bothered—I can always pay myself one. Take care, Walt"

Walt shook his head as he watched Tom turn and quickly disappeared. When Tom reached the parlor, he saw their weekend guest Penny Navarro sitting at the breakfast table. Penny lived in the Near-North Chicago area. She had a slim physical appearance, and her blue eyes had by a pair of brown Ben Franklin type glasses covering them. Her grey-brown knotted hair fit her current persona. She wore a pink tank top, a pair of Khaki pleated shorts, and Euro-designed, dark brown opened-toe sandals. Penny stayed at the B&B back in 2006. Tom liked her, but some of her ideas about life were a little hard to swallow. Penny studied metaphysical science.

"Hi Penny. So good to see you again. I missed you last night. Had to work later than usual last night."

"Hey Tom. Thank you. Dottie met me at the door. We sat and talked for a while. She told me you work for IBM now."

"Yes, IBM bought the company I worked for last month. I don't go to the office that much. I'm not into the corporate scene."

"I can tell, Tom. Most corporate types don't have Fu-Manchu beards. And they don't walk around in Hawaiian shirts and jeans. They must think you're from another world down there."

Tom laughed.

"Yeah, I'm pretty relaxed when it comes to appearance. I like to be comfortable in my own skin. You know what they say: Gray hair and a gray beard is God's graffiti."

Penny laughed.

"I know about gray hair, but not the grey beard. But I do pluck a few more chin hairs these days."

"So why are you here this time, Penny?"

"Well, I'm here to speak about reincarnation at the Spiritual University in town.

You know I'm a channel don't you?"

"Err, channel? I don't really understand what you mean by reincarnation. But if there is such a thing, I'd like to come back as my dogs. Not all at the same time."

"You know dogs think humans are God look-a-likes before they get here." The dogs' voice was lower this time.

Penny smiled.

"Some people believe we live more than one life. They think we die, and then come back as another person in another century. I am here to discuss the fact that all these lives are not in linear fashion — they occur simultaneously."

"So what you mean is if you don't succeed at life, keep on sucking at it until you do suck-seed!"
Penny had a strange look on her face.

"Oh. Let me explain a few things. The great energy of our essence dips in and out of time and space and becomes physical. We leave a life-trace as it dips in and out of specific present moments. In order to make sense of this process, we put these life-traces in linear form because our normal experience-patterns prevent a comprehensive view of these other lives. Am I making any sense to you, Tom?"

"I don't know if I believe everything I hear. You know the old saying about believing half of what you hear and none of what you see, right?"

"What do you mean, Tom?"

"Well, people don't know where information like this comes from. I use to say unverifiable facts and information are about as useful as sunscreen on a submarine. But I buy a lot more sunscreen these days. Thanks for the metaphysical meal. I'm off to my office to digest it."

Tom walked through the kitchen and onto the porch. Dottie made a bed on the floor next to his desk for Stallone.

"Well some things change, and some things don't, Dot."

"What are you talking about, Tom?"

"I just had a conversation with Penny. She may be way out there. I thought we wrote crazy guests off?"

"What is your take on her ideas about life, Tom?"

"Well, happy to answer the best way I knew how. I told her I didn't know if she was from this world, or just visiting."

Dottie looked up from the floor.
"People don't really care what we say or do. We can drift around the world free as a bird, or take a stand and express our self. Penny does that. She speaks, but someone in another world does the talking."

"Really Dot? So you think she's mostly dead and still talking?"

"Didn't you listen to her? Imagination and desire change the world. Besides there's a difference between mostly dead and all dead, Tom"

"You know I can't stay mad at someone that is smart and makes me laugh. Penny has a brilliant and funny personality, but some of her ideas can be a little annoying."

208

"I know Tom. Everything in California annoys you. You better make that appointment with Rhonda soon. Your health is about to stress me out."

Tom took a seat at the computer. As he did, he felt a twinge in his chest.

"Never felt better, but who knows about the rest of these flakes out here. They like to rip a perfectly good life apart. You know that don't you, Dot?"

"But you know what they say—your beliefs make that so in your world."

"Who are they, Dot?"

"Well, "the they" is Penny. You know she speaks as a group? Penny came here to throw little bits of fiery information out to the public, so they can come out of the dark ages of half-truths."

Tom wanted to get some work done. He wanted to end the conversation about Penny, so he used a typical Tom tactic.

"Suppose you felt crazy and suppose you were Penny. Here I go repeating myself. It must be one of my other life traces that Penny talked about. We cross moments, and both of us speak at the same time."

Chapter 17

If you can't get rid of the family skeleton, you may as well make it dance.

George Bernard Shaw

"People say Islam is the "Religion of Peace." If Iraq and Afghanistan believe in Islam, I think they need to read the English definition of peace.""

Hazel was on one of her liquor induced rants at the B&B one weekend in August, 2012. Tom, Dottie, Ruth, Todd and Hazel and Ruth's latest flame, Desmond Barnes, sat around the dining table discussing the fate of the world after one of Dottie's famous fried chicken dinners. The years didn't mellow Hazel's attitude much, but they did add several pounds to her stocky frame.

The age lines, and wrinkles made her look older than her fifty-six years. When she opened her mouth, all hope of her acting as a rational, fun-loving middle-age woman quickly disappeared. Her cynical view about Muslims and their faith was just one of the topics she liked to rant about in front of an audience—especially if the audience included family members.
Ruth was the first to counter Hazel's thoughts.

"War isn't one sided, Hazel. Christians and Jews distort the peace by accepting war. Fighting is in our blood.

Christians and Jews accept the taking of a human life. They don't even give it a second thought. But if someone abuses a household pet they become villains. I believe they both represent our lack of compassion for life."

Dottie shook her head.

"That's right, Ruth. Killing each other and justifying it through our religious groups is what we do. Look how Christianity started. The Jews and the Romans killed Christ, and then a bunch of zealots decided to make a religion out of it. It took them a while to get the thing going. But with a little fiction, and a lot of fear they made it work. Living in fear for the last two thousand years seems to be our saving grace. We call that grace, religion."

Hazel took a healthy sip of her hazelnut coffee laced with Drambuie, and Tom opened his mouth.

"I wonder what year Jesus thought it was?"

Hazel got emotional when she heard that comment.

"You're not funny, Tom. And that's not the real story. The apostles had to form a religion to protect themselves and their followers."

Tom got serious.

"The apostles were a bunch of misfits. They didn't even stay around to watch the crucifixion. There were other texts written at the time that claim Christ's death was not a real event. Those old texts say some other guy took his place."

Haze's temper caught fire.

"That's heresy at its finest, Tom. The apostles couldn't bear the thought of seeing Jesus die."

Dottie spoke up.

"That's the point, Hazel. They didn't know what to do. They feared everything, and they used a bunch of bullshit to make that fear stronger."

Hazel didn't let the battle die.

"You can't talk like that, Dot. Have you lost your faith in God? Have you lost your sense of right and wrong? If not for religion, we would all be worshiping grasshoppers and spiders."

Tom had to continue the conversation.

"If you feed a starving dog and make it well, it will not bite you. We can't say the same thing about humans." The dogs' sounded peaceful this time.

"I think everyone should be treated like Christians. But don't blame me for the consequences, Hazel. The only good thing to come out of all these religions is the music. God and religion are strange bedfellows, Hazel. God is not something to fear, and God is certainly not something to fight about. God is something to experience in our own way."

Just the thought of Tom getting the upper hand in the conversation made Hazel's blood boil.

"That's crazy talk, but I shouldn't expect any more from you, Tom. Should I?"

"Hazel, you don't want to hear what other people think. You don't even what to hear what your husband thinks. All you want to hear is what you think in a different tone. That doesn't work for me."

Dottie quickly changed to subject.

"How are the kids, Todd?"

"Fine. I guess. Lois is in some kind of hell over in Europe, and Eddie works for me."

Ruth had to ask.

"What is some kind of hell, Todd?"

"She lives in England with a musician. Every time we talk to her we ask her what she likes doing. And she said she worked on some kind of hell last night. Hazel asked her what she meant, and Lois said she and her boyfriend put together an album, and the title is — "Some Kind of Hell.""

Ruth started to laugh, and so did Desmond.

"Sounds heavy, Hazel. Did you listen to any cuts from this album?"

Hazel felt the buzz as she finished her coffee.

"I don't give a shit about that kind of music. It sounds like devil music."

Dottie laughed.

"See, Hazel. You want to fight over something you don't like. You care less whether your daughter likes it. You look at your side, and call it the right side. We all like to do that. We always strive for right. But some of us realize growth and change are in the confusion we create."

Hazel threw her napkin on the table.

"Let's go upstairs, Todd. I need a hot bath."

Todd started to get up. As he pushed himself out of the armed chair he realized his drunken state. The two double scotches before dinner, and the three glasses of wine with dinner, put him way over his limit. He put his arm around his wife.

"Do you want me to rub your back, honey?"

Hazel pushed him away, and shook her head from side-to-side. She almost fell over his chair as she did.

Ruth's head felt like a spinning top. But she got up and looked at Hazel.

"Why don't you and Todd come to our room? I want you to get to know Desmond a little better."

Hazel looked at Ruth with disdain.

"Are you kidding Ruth? Keep your sex games to yourself.

Tom had to comment.

"Come on Ruth? We have another guest up there. We can't afford any more of your free love episodes. You know what happened the last time?"

Ruth had a smile on her face.

"Do you mean last year when the cops stayed here?"

"One cop said he heard moans all night long. He told me that you had sex all night with the other cop."

"Yeah, I know. I gave them both my number the next morning. I still here from them. Been too busy to fool with them."

Desmond didn't say much at the table. He seemed to enjoy the family debate. Ruth introduced him as her young flight attendant from San Francisco. But he looked more like a thirty-year old farmer from Kansas. Ruth's honesty didn't seem to bother him, but he did have something to say.

"Let's get some sleep tonight, Ruth. I, too, feel a little out of it."

Ruth's glassy eyes told the story. She grabbed him between the legs. She rubbed her hand up and down his crotch several times.

"Okay, baby. I guess all that talk about the cops made you horny, and you want me all to yourself."

Desmond pulled her hand away. He suspected she was a sex maniac, but now he knew she was. He met Ruth two days before in a bar on the Warf in San Francisco. They had sex the first night and the next. Ruth convinced him to drive her to Willits. He had four days off, so he decided the trip would be a mini-vacation. He thought she was a cougar, and that didn't bother him. The sex maniac part changed his opinion of her. Desmond decided that this would be their last date.

"I've got to get back for a flight on Tuesday, so I need to get some sleep."

Tom had to push the knife in a little further. Desmond looked like a reasonable guy; not a sex pervert.

"You came with the wrong person if want to sleep, Desmond."

"Yeah, I guess you're right, Tom. But it takes two to tango if you know what I mean?"

"Not with Ruth, buddy. She has more steps than the Empire State Building."

Desmond laughed as Ruth pulled him away from Tom. She gave Tom the finger as she left the dining room.

Dottie looked at Tom.

"How can I have so many skeletons in my family closet,

Tom?"

Tom smiled as he walked into the kitchen with an armful of dishes.

"They walked out of your mental closet years ago, honey. No one has a big enough closet to hold a pair of walking cadavers like them. I think those Zombies would thrive in another life. By the way, who is the other guest tonight? I didn't get a chance to introduce myself."

"Oh no. Let's not start that reincarnation stuff again. The guest seems very nice. She said she reports the news. She came here to do some sort of story on our B&B, I think. Fortunately, she went to dinner with a friend that lives in Ukiah. By the time she gets back, my crazy family should be asleep."

"We can only hope and pray, Dot. You know Zombies don't like to sleep."

"Stop, Tom. Please, go get the glasses from the table so we can go to bed. I'm exhausted."

The next morning Ashley Moore's alarm went off at eight. She slept like a rock in that old Victorian home. That was the feedback she got from three of her friends who stayed there last year. Her friends told her to do a story in the Chronicle about the B&B, so other San Francisco couples could enjoy a weekend or a special occasion there. She liked being a reporter. The San Francisco Chronicle rocked, even though the circulation is in a nosedive was. Her job was to find interesting articles for the living section of the paper. The President B&B came up in a meeting two weeks earlier. The editor found out about the B&B from his daughter. She and her husband celebrated their fifth anniversary there and loved it. During the meeting, Ashley brought up what she heard about the place, so the editor gave her the assignment. Her mission was to write an article about the home as well as the owners. That kind of writing is in her literary DNA. By the time she got herself together, it was 8:40. She grabbed her phone and recorder, and opened the nine-foot bedroom door.

As she walked down the old stairs, she saw a man standing on the front steps. It was Tom. He and Stallone just came back from their morning walk around the neighborhood. Tom had a phone in his ear talking to Jack on his way out of town. Ashley opened the front door.

"Good morning. Are you Mr. Donovan?"

Before Tom could answer, Ashley put her hand out, so Stallone could get acquainted with her. And then she stooped down to hug him.

"Yes. Call me Tom. You must be the reporter Dottie told me you want to write about the B&B. Thank you. We could use a little positive press."

Ashley stood up and put her hand out to Tom.

"I'm Ashley Moore. I hear a lot of great things about this place. I'm on my way to the dining room for breakfast."

"Great. Dottie made something special this morning. I know you'll love it."

Tom and Stallone quickly went in to the entrance foyer and pulled the keys off the antique pegboard that doubled as a key holder. Once he found the keys, he tried to keep up with Ashley before she sat down.

Ashley stood by the table admiring some of Iris's pottery when Tom entered.

"Take any seat Ashley. We do have other guests, but I doubt we'll see them before 11. They are family members and they like to sleep in."

Tom crossed his fingers behind his back. The last thing he needed was that group putting their two cents in about the B&B. He never knew what Hazel or Ruth would say because they didn't know themselves. Dottie came out of the kitchen with her signature morning smoothie.

"Good morning Ashley. I made Cinnamon Polenta Pancakes this morning. I top them with strawberries and blueberries. How about a smoothie to start?"

"Perfect, Dottie. The smoothie sounds great. Can I have a cup of tea, please."

"Mint or Earl Gray Black Full Leaf?"

"Earl Gray works."

Ashley's eyes cruised around the room looking at the memorabilia strategically placed in perfect balance. Tom stood by the kitchen door with Stallone lying next to the him.

"When did you buy the B&B, Tom?"

Tom thought for a minute.

"Over twenty years ago. It's a great house in a wonderful town. I'm no fan of California, but Willits does have its strong points."

"What's wrong with California?"

"You know the usual things. When we enter this world, we get a free ticket to a freak show. When you live in California, you get a seat in the first row."

Ashley came from and still lived in Walnut Creek, one of the exclusive suburbs of Oakland. Her California girl roots came through and through. But she laughed at Tom's comment.

Dottie came out of the kitchen with tea and tried to trump Tom's comments

"Oh, we love Willits and California. Tom gets a little frustrated with some of the crazy laws in this state. But overall this is a wonderful place to live and raise our kids."

Ashley put a slice of lemon in her tea and took a sip. She put the antique china cup down and looked at Tom.

"Yeah, some laws do challenge common sense, but Brown is doing his best to get the state on the right track."

Tom knew it. The Chronicle was one of the most liberal newspapers in the country. He felt his stomach tighten.

"I like to turn painful situations around using humor. I try to find humor in everything, but that's hard to do when we talk about California politics."

Ashley felt Tom's dislike for the topic. Oh, I'm not here to talk about politics. I write for the living section of the paper. I want to hear about you, and Dot, and your beautiful B&B."

Dottie brought the pancakes out, and she put a small pot of tea on the table. She left the room and signaled Tom to leave too, but he stood by the door and continued the conversation.

"We want to share our experiences with you. Our guest log has over five hundred names so far, and many of them come back every year. The ones that don't come back usually stay in touch in one way or another. Off course we had some really crazy folks visit, and they never come back. Crazy folks like family members always come back."

Ashley smiled. "I bet you meet some interesting people."

Dottie had to add her thoughts before Tom could throw some verbal cold water on this free advertising fire.

"Thanks to that journal, we plan to write a book about the

B&B when we retire."

"Great I want to buy a copy when you do."

Dottie spent the next three hours telling Ashley about the B&B, and the people that became friends as well as just guests. Tom would interject his thoughts from time to time, and for the most part they tethered on the positive. Ashley looked at her Fossil watch and turned her recorder off.

"Well, I think I have enough material to write a great article. I do want to take some pictures and walk around town. I also want to meet a neighbor or two if that's okay? I should start heading home around four, so I better get on it. I want to get this in print form as soon as possible."

Tom got up from the table and put out his hand.

I'm sure the neighbors would like to talk to a reporter from the Chronicle, especially old Walt."

"Who is old Walt, Tom?"

"He's a big fan of your paper. He reads it every day, and we argue about what he reads after he reads it."

"Oh, you don't read our paper?"

"No, but Walt fills me in, if there's something worthwhile to read."

Ashley didn't know how to take that comment, so she ignored it.

"Sounds like old Walt is a good friend."

"Friends like Walt talk a lot of nonsense. I might not agree with all of it, but he knows I respect his love for nonsense."

"Sounds like a new take on the word friendship, Tom."

"I trust my faith in fools; Walt calls it self-confidence."

Ashley laughed and walked toward the entrance hall. As she did, Ruth came down the steps.

"Did I miss breakfast?"

Tom looked at her as Ashley walked out the front door.

"You never miss anything around here, Ruth especially if it has to do with eating and drinking."

"Oh kiss my ass, Tom. You know I only eat when I'm sexually starved."

Tom turned his back and started to blow her comment off, but he couldn't help himself.

"Yeah, you look famished!"

If no knows when a person is going to die, how can we say he died prematurely?

George Carlin

You thought you could fix you. But what you didn't understand was your ego decided you couldn't fix yourself. We call that a camouflaged belief.

You tried to convince yourself you could heal your body, but you forgot how to do it. You forgot to listen to your inner self. You lived in physical fear. Fear is a very strange energy. It turns your body into a war zone, and the consciousness within the cells weaken from the stress of that war.

Chapter 18

That's what happens when the "Big One" comes. You go to bed fine, then you wake up dead.

Red Fox

Ashley's article didn't appear in the Chronicle the following Sunday. Tom kept checking Walt's Sunday paper, but nothing that resembled Ashley writing project surfaced. The article finally appeared the first week of November, 2012 exactly one month before Tom's 58th birthday. The Headline read:

There's Nothing Better Than A Friend Unless It Is A Friend That Owns The President B&B in Willits.

Walt saw the article that Sunday morning. He quickly crossed the small street between his house and the B&B. The unlocked side door made it easy to walk in and head straight to the kitchen. Dottie quickly cut greens for the turtle while turning to greet Walt.

"Hey Dottie. Where's Tom? That reporter chick finally put the article in the paper."

Walt tried to put the living section of the paper on the dirty kitchen counter.

"Oh wait, Walt. Let me clean the lettuce off first."

Dottie quickly push the mess to one side as Tom walked in from the porch. Tom stood next to Walt.

"Finally! She took her sweet time about it. Did you read it, Walt?"

Walt smiled.

"Hell yes. I read it. I looked at the picture first. The outside shot of the house shows a small portion of our house in the picture. Millie got a kick out of that. Brick and Dena came over, and they read it too."

Tom looked at Walt with one of his "what the hell looks. "

"Sounds like the whole town of Willits saw it before we did."

Walt laughed. "Guess you should think about getting the Sunday instead of boycotting the paper, Tom"

"Not in this life, buddy. I have my hands full with you and Jack when it comes to liberal antics."

Tom watched Walt as he pointed to the picture of Dottie in her B&B apron. Like a true B&B queen, she stood by the dining room table with a smile on her face —and a smoothie in her hand.

Jack walk through the front door and join the group in the kitchen. Jack laughed when he saw Tom standing on the front steps next to the "Welcome Sign."

"Hey Tom. Never thought I would see you standing next to any kind of welcome sign in this state."

Tom smiled. "I know, right? I look like a lawyer with that smile on my face. Anyone who smiles like that must want to sell you something you don't need."

The room broke up. Tom could still look at himself and laugh.

"God Tom can you believe you're fifty-eight?"

Dottie and the girls gathered around the dining room table to celebrate another birthday.

Tom smirked as the words "fifty-eight" flowed out of his wife's mouth.

"The scary part of getting older comes with knowing members of my high school class could be running the country now. This nightmare happens often. You know what I mean?" The girls laughed. Iris was the first to speak.

"From what you told us all those characters' act like criminals, dad."

"Right. The guys running the country act the same way."

The group laughed again.

"I guess I should start each day with my pomegranate-blueberry juice and the obituaries now."

"Don't be silly, Tom. Most of your friends have to catch up to you age wise. Fifty-eight is what some folks call "prime time" these days. You have good genes. Look at your dad. The man is a rock at ninety-two. Well, maybe a stone is more like it."

Dottie didn't like to talk about dying. Joking about getting older helped ease the fear of death. But just the thought of Tom dying sent a bolt of fear through her body. She knew he didn't look well. She knew he would not go to the doctor — the B&B king has his own plan when it came to health. She tried everything she could to get him to eat better and exercise more, but Tom continued to be that Tom. Even an act of congress would not convince him to alter his mental and physical regime.

"Just remember, girls; I believe old age will always be twenty years older than I am."

Erica liked that. "Keep thinking that way, dad. Fifty-eight is the youth of old age, right."

"You better believe it, Kiddo. Mark Twain always said: Age is an issue of mind over matter. If you don't mind it doesn't matter. I second that thought!"

Tiffany wanted to call her boyfriend, so she hurried the family party along.

"Hey, let's sing Happy Birthday! I want to call Josh.

"Tiffany, it's only 7:30. Do he go to bed early? He must feel older than me."

"Dad! He went to see his folks in Boston. You know, the time change messes with phone calls."

"Oh. Thank God. I thought you started dating a really old man."

Tiffany gave her dad an off the shoulder look.

"That's funny, dad. That is real funny!"

The group ate the chocolate mousse cake. They sat around the table telling stories about growing up. The girls wanted to hear about Tom's youth. They thought he qualified as a true maverick.

"You know the great part of getting older girls?"

Tiffany answered.

"What's that dad?"

"I can get out of all those boring social events around town just by saying I'm tired."

The girls laughed and Dottie shook her head in agreement.

"I can't believe the New Year came and went, Tom. It seems like 2012 only had six months in it. Can you believe it's almost Valentine's Day 2013?"

Tom sat at his computer feeling a little sick. He heard Dottie's words, but he had a hard time focusing on her words.

"What's that, Dot?"

Dottie got use to repeating herself.

"I said the turtle just ate all the chickens."

"Hold on. Let me finish this one report, and I'll go take a look."

"Really, Tom? Get a grip will-ya, please."

Tom tried to finish an IBM project due the next day, but his indigestion made him lose focus again. Dottie's words made no sense, so he had to do something. He closed the document, got up, and walked into the kitchen.

"I need a couple of Rolaids. Do we have any?"

Dottie opened the lower cabinet, and started to push pill bottles and other remedies around until she found the antacid pills.

"Here. Are you okay?" Dottie could tell he was not himself.

"I'm fine. I think that vegan salad you fixed last night gave me indigestion."

"You didn't eat any of it, Tom."

"I know. Just looking at it made my stomach sick."

Dottie smiled and shook her head.

Well, I hope you start to feel better because we have a full house this week because of Valentine Day. Lots of calls from the bay area all of a sudden. The article Ashley printed a couple of months ago really helped our business. All of next week's guests know each other, so prepare for the busy time around here night and day."

"Don't worry. I'll be in top shape by this afternoon."

Valentine week was hectic, but the guests were gracious and normal by Tom standards. Bookings slowed down last the week in February. Dottie only booked one guest for that week. The guest, Ernie Ewald, from Pennsylvania, was a friend of Tom's family. When Ernie arrived the morning of the 27th, Tom met him at the door.

"Hey Ernie! What brings you out to La-La Land? Whatever it is I'm glad you made it here. Are you hungry? Dottie has coffee and muffins ready."

"Thanks Tom. It's good to see you. It looks like California agrees with you. You look like a well-fed hippie. Coffee sounds good."

"Okay, but watch your tongue. Getting rid of hippies is one of my goals. But nothing works. No even crosses and garlic."

Ernie laughed, and so did Tom as they walked into the dining room. Ernie sat at the head of the table, and Tom stood by the kitchen door. Tom started the conversation.

"The last time I talked to dad he said you got real sick. You look great now."

"I had a by-pass operation. Well, it was quadruple bypass surgery, and I feel great."

"I can tell. How old are you now, Ernie?"

Before Ernie could answer Dottie came out of the kitchen with muffins and coffee. She gave Ernie a hug and kissed him on the cheek. She grabbed his arm as he reached for the coffee.

"You look great, Ernie. I happy you're staying with us."

"Thanks, Dot. You know I just turned eighty. They say eighty is the new sixty."

Tom shook his head in agreement. "I feel sixty too, Ernie."

"Do you have health issues, Tom? Go see a doctor. I didn't want to go, but my oldest daughter forced me to go. I wanted to stop feeling so bad. The indigestion, lack of energy, and shortness of breath really puts a dent in my lifestyle. You know I have a two-handicap, don't you? I had a hard time playing, and that really got under my skin."

Dottie listened to Ernie's symptoms and immediately put two and two together. Tom must have a couple of blocked arteries. She had to do something. Ernie might be able to help her convince Tom that he needed medical help.

"You know Tom complains of the same sort of symptoms, and he refuses to see our doctor. Can you pound some sense into that stubborn head of his?"

"The surgery wasn't that bad, Tom. Six to eight-weeks recovery time. Don't wait until it's too late get some help, boy."

Tom looked at Dottie and then at Ernie. He could see the fear in his wife's eyes. And he felt the fear surrounding his own body. But, he had a plan, and he seemed stuck to it.

"Dot I'm better than I was a year ago, and I'll be better than I am a year from now. I have a long term plan. You just have to trust me."

"Never mind your long term plan. I'm making an appointment with Rhonda."

"Okay, but I can't go until next Thursday. I have a big program to write this week."

"I'm not kidding, Tom. You gotta go next week for sure." Tom worked on his new program and finished it on the Wednesday before his appointment. That afternoon, Stallone and Tom took a nap. They usually slept for a little over an hour, but on this day, time had another plan.

Tom did what his nephew said he did years before: "He forgot to wake up."

And Stallone followed his master.

The dogs'voice felt closer now.

"*In life we are your friend, your defender and your soul mate. We are faithful and true to the last beat of your heart and eternally ever after.*

Epilogue

I think we're part of a greater wisdom that we will ever understand; a higher order, call it what you want. Know what I call it? The Big Electron. It doesn't punish, it doesn't reward, it doesn't judge at all. It just is."

George Carlin

Tom didn't watch anymore. His new image fit his mind in the region of choices. He had more choices to make. But he could rest and recuperate, if he felt the desire to do so. Desire is a key emotional thought just like it in physical life. Ideas and images bounced through his vivacious spirit, and he started to focus on his dream reality. Was he dreaming now? Or, was his physical reality a dream? Where do these realities start and stop? Perhaps dreams don't have a beginning or ending. Perhaps life is a concurrent dream that expands our awareness with or without a physical body. Dreams may serve as a foundation for other regions of consciousness.

Tom heard George's voice again.

"Most of our species believed we are alone in the universe. I guess they believed that the universe aimed rather low and settled for very little. When I was physical, I tried to believe that there is a God who created each of us in His own image and likeness and that he loved us very much and kept a close eye on things. I really tried to believe that, but

I gotta tell you, the longer I lived, the more I looked around. Then I realized that someone or something was fucked up. How can God be perfect? Everything he makes dies."

Tom felt the joy. After all, he told himself what George liked to tell himself. He felt another one coming:

"You know The Human Species could have been super human, but instead we were satisfied with lights on our tennis shoes."

Tom didn't need lights on his tennis shoes anymore. He was a non-physical electromagnetic light show now.

About The Author

There's no denying it. My physical personality was lost in one crazy bad-ass netherworld of misremembering for the first forty-seven years of my life. My inner personality kept getting body-slammed by my physical one while I built my egocentric world. I like to say I was a religious, capitalistic slave, immersed in a vat of distorted values. And here's the thing: that is a realistic description of the physical image I created through years of business conditioning and knee-jerk personal choices.

I was a hardheaded, egotistical college dropout with doctoral-level personality skills. My goal was to sell my way to fame and glory, one shoe at a time. I was a money-hungry young shoe salesman—a shoe salesman willing to do the low-class ego dance for an order. I had the capitalistic brazenness to move up the corporate shoe ladder.

My capitalistic persona would always stretch reason-ability to its outer limits. So when I failed a time or two or three, I blamed the system. But I rose from my self-created ashes and got objectively successful again by selling more than one shoe at a time. I was selling container loads of shoes at one time. And once I felt successful, I wanted more power and more recognition.

When I bet it all with a blundering, alcohol-enriched mind I offered my impressive shoe talents to the capitalistic wolves, expecting to become one. But my narrow-minded focus sent me over the cliff of self-discovery. My physical personality was in free fall, and all my lifelines burned in a fire I made. My reality started to change, and I started to feel another presence within me. My inner personality guided me to the bottom, so I could internally heal my self-imposed wounds.

Once I hit bottom, my physical personality drifted in a mysterious mixture of self-pity and irrelevance. But my inner personality came to the rescue. The energy within my inner personality took over when my mother passed in

1996. And that personality helped me understand the passing of my younger brother, Bob, and my dad, Howard, in 2013. I felt something special during these monumental losses. It felt like I was standing in a nonphysical stream of understanding, and I felt the pure energy in that understanding.

My physical personality followed that stream when I began reading psychology and philosophy books. I found Rumi quotes in many of those books, so at forty-seven, I bought my first book of poetry. The *Essential Rumi* by Coleman Barks introduced me to some of his thoughts. Rumi, the thirteenth-century Sufi mystic, is an inner-self shaker. I started to look at the nonphysical part of things because of Rumi.

Then Confucius, Lao Tzu, Buddha, the German Poet Rainer Maria Rilke, and William Blake gave me their versions of inner personality expressions. Jesus, Muhamad, Ralph Waldo Emerson, Ernest Holmes, James Allen, and other soul-seekers through the ages all said the same thing. And they all used their inner personalities to say it.

By the time I found Japan's Shinkichi Takahashi's work, I was on the edge of a nonphysical bridge. I realized that I'd been on that bridge all my physical life but ignored being there. I'd always felt the presence of an agreeable being in my thoughts. But I rarely paid attention to that being until I read Ask and It Is Given as soon as it hit the bookstores.

Abraham, the author of the book, is a nonphysical energy

239

personality who expresses common sense thoughts about the nature of physical life.

Then I hit the jackpot when I found the Seth Material. Jane Roberts, the poet and writer, brought the thoughts of non-physical Seth into my world during my fifties. When Elias and Zurac came into my life in the first decade of the twenty-first century through the internet and a booth at Nashville's Galactic Expo, I realized that these nonphysical personalities' unfiltered messages were helping me forge an unfiltered path on this physical journey.

 What I've learned on this journey is that I am here to physically experience my thoughts, emotions, perceptions, and choices. I know now what the sages and the people who used their inner senses in this reality were trying to tell me and everyone else: Our thoughts and emotions are forms of energy that act like cells when we project them into our reality using a mechanism we call "perception." They are the tools we use to create what we experience physically.

 I'm not here to form a group or write sermons about self-responsibility. And I'm not here to act like someone who crossed the self-awareness finish line and is basking in a state of bliss. My physical personality is still physically focused on creating my reality. But I'm increasingly using my inner personality to do it. I live in more than one reality. And I'm just beginning to appreciate what these other realities do for me.